Stephen McGeagh was born in Liverpool in 1981, and moved to Manchester a few years later. He studied English at MMU, before returning as a postgraduate to their Writing School. *Habit* is his first novel.

HABIT

STEPHEN McGEAGH

CROMER

PUBLISHED BY SALT PUBLISHING
12 Norwich Road, Cromer, Norfolk NR27 0AX United Kingdom

© Stephen McGeagh 2012

The right of Stephen McGeagh to be identified as the author of this work
has been asserted by him in accordance with Section 77 of the Copyright,
Designs and Patents Act 1988.

This book is in copyright. Subject to statutory exception and to provisions
of relevant collective licensing agreements, no reproduction of any part may
take place without the written permission of Salt Publishing.

First published by Salt Publishing, 2012

Printed in the UK by TJ International Ltd, Padstow, Cornwall

Typeset in Paperback 9.5 / 14.5

*This book is sold subject to the conditions that it shall not, by way of trade
or otherwise, be lent, re-sold, hired out, or otherwise circulated without the
publisher's prior consent in any form of binding or cover other than that in which
it is published and without a similar condition including this condition being
imposed on the subsequent purchaser.*

ISBN 978 1 97773 33 4 paperback

1 3 5 7 9 8 6 4 2

For Laura

1

The kid on the pavement, eyeballing me, spits as the bus sets off. I'm sat on that seat on the bottom deck. Over the back wheels. High enough. Scanning down to the driver, checking who's getting on and off. Sat there because when she gets on I'll be able to scope her out again. Well nice. Fit as.

I'm on my way to sign on a couple of weeks ago, hungover like a motherfucker, in this very seat, and she gets on. Shows her pass and walks down the aisle to find somewhere to sit and all I can think is I hope she can't smell my breath because she'll probably fucking die if she can, and how pretty is she?

I pull my hood up a bit more because we're about to get to her stop and I don't want her to clock me and think I'm trying to get a look at her again. Just so happens this is dole day. Yeah, I always get the bus at this time, what of it? Least my head's clear today. Couldn't have a drink or anything last night because I went to see Mand and she kept me there for ages and made me some tea. Watched some right shit on the telly, stuck the washing machine on with a bagful in there, brewed up, hung the washing up. I was too bored to have a beer by then. Bare knackered just watching her. Kipped there and everything. Fair enough though. What's your big sister for if not to wipe your backside? Tell her that and she'd proper belt me. The bus turns right and brakes. Just outside the shops and that bird's not even at the stop. What a waste of my time.

The day is shit. The rain drops are leaving dirty, greasy, streaks on the windows and people are racing around outside, taking big steps over puddles. We pull up at the next stop and an old woman hobbles up to the driver, unzips the top of her shopping trolley and starts rooting around for a purse or a pass or something. I can see the people in the queue behind her wishing they'd got on first and not tried to look good by being polite and letting the old girl on. There's no shelter at the stop and one woman, who put her brolly down when she saw the bus, starts to put it back up again. Her face is hard and I can see the slag-line of make-up round her chin from where I'm sitting so it must look like a fucking orange cliff close up. She gets her leopard-print umbrella back up then the queue starts to move so it's down again and her black eyes follow the old bird down the aisle. Wonder if you put them in a room together right now, door locked, no consequences, what would hard face do? I reckon nothing. People love looking angry. We cane it off again at a breakneck twenty and I can see the gym that used to be a bingo hall that used to be a cinema looking across the traffic island that marks the start of Sale town centre. The island's got a footpath across it, some grass and bushes, but the green on them is off. Dirty like the windows. I wipe the inside of the glass with my sleeve and it comes back wet and cold. I get off next so I ring the bell and quickly get past the old bird who's getting up – one stop for fuckssake – and wait for the doors to open. The rain's gone off a bit but I can hear it on my hood when I step down onto the pavement. The courts are on my left and I walk to the crossing. It's got red brick ramps on the sides and dark windows, cigarette bins on every bit of wall, cigarette ends on the floor underneath covered in dabs of spit. I still want to run up the ramps, chase Mand up and back down, up and down, shitting it in case someone comes out and drags us in to see a judge. Need to get a grip of that. Not a kid now.

Not bothered with a green man today, the road's pretty quiet so I get over onto the pedestrian bit quick. First there's a load of estate agents, all huddled together on the edge of the main set of shops. I never understood how so many can go on, all put up against each other. I can smell roast chicken coming from a butcher's a bit further on. The precinct slopes up a hill to the met stop and after a bit I get past Boot's and I'm at the next crossing and I'm sur-rounded by banks. On my way to the bank. Sort of. Mand reckons her rent is well too high but she pays it because she doesn't want to drop off the radar. Taking every hour they'll give her at work just to keep a tiny house, on a shitty road. She says I'm dropping off. Dig and me got it sussed ages ago. Rent free over his uncle's shop. No heating, no cash, no problem. The crossing is waiting for me at the top end, green all the way to the other side, and I give a girl in a Mini a nod while she's waiting at the lights. I hear her speed off when I get across, probably giving me the finger. The tram stop's just at the top of the hill, waiting for me with its new yellow signs. They were all about grey and green at first. I even think I can remember when trains still went down these tracks but that might be something my brain's made up. A false memory. In the paper they said your best memories from being a kid are probably lies. The stuff you try to hang onto when things are getting the most fucking raw and you can't see past your own screaming – oh, by the way, that stuff never happened. Over the road, still on the hill but opposite the tram, is the town hall and round the corner there's a library and a theatre that I've never been to, and I only know that they're there anyway because they're next to pubs. I duck into the tram station and go past the ticket machines on my way down the pigeon-shit-covered steps to the empty platform.

The rain slides off the sloped roof on the opposite side and down onto the rocks and rubbish all over the tracks. I can see a few battered papers down there, that must get dropped when people squeeze themselves onto the proper hammered trams in the early morning. Mand says you can't breathe on there sometimes. When it's winter and wet, and no one wants to crack a window, especially not some fucker who's *already* got a seat and doesn't want the wind to whip past his headphones; when it's like that she says you can't breathe and the air is thick like blood. You choke on there, she reckons. A tram glides into the station on it s way to town, on the other platform, not my way. A girl is sitting in the back half, so she's travelling backwards, and she keeps staring at me as the thing moves off. I wipe my nose with my sleeve. The grey day means the trams have their headlights on, so I know there's one coming as it's easy to spot in the distance. On the green metal bench by the wall behind me there's another old girl messing with her bag, scrabbling about for something like mad. Her hands are dipping in and out, scratching like chicken's feet, and she's muttering some weird shit.

'Where's my pass?'

She's asking me, because there's no one else about. The noise from the road back up the stairs has gone. I walk a bit further down the platform and lean out at the edge a bit to check if the tram's any closer. Nearly here.

'I had it just there, with my purse and my letters.' She starts to get up.

I keep walking, backwards, facing her but watching the tram pull in.

'How am I going to get around without it?' She shakes her head and turns towards the stairs.

I press the button to open the doors seven times before anything happens, then I get on and sit up near the front and pull the strings of my hood so it's tight around my face.

Two women get on and sit behind me. I can see them reflected in the glass panel on the driver's cabin in front of me. They smell like wet cigs. One of them looks older than she probably is, and her face is angry.

'I'd feel sorry for them, but they've always got to have about six kids. Who needs six kids?'

The younger-looking one screws her face up like she's smelt shit.

'I know, poor little bastards. Born into that arsehole, and it's only going to get worse now for them.' She's got long hair, tied up, and she's got a mole on her neck.

'Ah fuck them. What can you do?' Older crosses her arms over her chest. 'Seen those pictures of our Reece's little 'un? Doesn't she look like him?'

The dole office is only about ten minutes away, on the edge of Altrincham, but the rain makes it seem further. The women bob in and out of my view in the glass and the tram bounces along the track, and I keep losing the conversation because of the sound of the rails outside. I get my phone out of my pocket and mash the numbers with my thumb to make the back-light come on without unlocking it. 11:02 and no messages. I've got a picture of some bird and her fake tits as my wallpaper. The operator logo cuts right across her face so I can't tell if she's pretty or not, I can't see her eyes. I don't know how it even got there. Maybe Dig did it. I unlock the keypad and press through to my saved messages. There's one, and I read it slowly then tuck my phone back inside my jacket. When I look up the two women have gone and all the seats behind me in the carriage are empty.

The tram slows down and stops and the doors slide open and the platform is empty but I can see someone standing in the doorway of the newsagents, down the far end. There's a bike locked up on the railings, a proper shitty one that no one would steal if it wasn't locked up, and I feel like I want to kick it on the way past. I get past the shop quickly but I'm not quick enough because I hear the man's voice loud in my right ear.

'Michael, lad, you all right?'

I don't answer, just tuck my hands into my sleeves and do a quickstep down the ramp to the road, sort of the kind where you kick your legs that bit faster when you're walking and you think it's sped you up, but it fucking hasn't. I can see the office tower block already in the distance, and it almost makes me turn back, the thought of sitting in there for an hour getting grilled and not having real answers except that I want money for nothing so just fucking give it to me, and no I haven't applied for those thirty shite jobs you gave me because they wouldn't take me on if I did, and if they did then I'd fuck it off after a few days because I don't want to fucking work. Straight up. Some little kid is running around his front garden screaming his fucking head off and banging on the grass and on his wall with a bit of copper pipe but he stops when he sees me walking past and just stares at me.

I'm still a bit away from the job centre doors but I can hear some screaming already. Probably some mad bitch going off her nut about child benefit. I can see a bloke standing outside and his cigarette is just hanging from his hand like he's forgotten about it, like it's going to drop half-smoked on the floor any minute. He's watching the big automatic double doors, and when I get up near him I start watching them too. The shouting hasn't stopped but I can't make out the words until the doors slide back and a fat security guard carries out this girl who looks about twelve but she's raging, kicking out everywhere. Her foot just misses my face as they fall down the path, the guard with his bear hug around her waist bending his head and neck back so he doesn't get one of her elbows in the gob. They get to the roadside and he dumps her on her arse and steps back quick. She spins round to face him and she's a mad cat, staring him down.

'Bastard!' she screams at him. 'Bastards!' she screams at the job centre concrete. The security guard and the building are both quiet, and then he just turns away and walks back inside like nothing happened, like he does it every day. The doors slide shut behind him. The girl spits on the pavement but I can't see where it lands because the ground's wet from the rain.

Inside there's a queue. A few scally lads. A big boy with eyes that don't point where he wants them to. A girl who looks scared, with a grey coat wrapped all around her, and her hands can't stop messing in the pockets. There's an old fella with a face on, sat down, who probably doesn't even care about the queue. The longer he sits there, the longer it is til he goes home to start crying. I start waiting. One of the lads looks round at me and grins a bit, like they do when they reckon you're no trouble. He nudges his mate and they both look round then. I look at my boots. They're black, and dirty, and look dirtier next to the clean green carpet in the centre. When I look up they're not staring any more. I open my fists. I get to the desk.

'Name?'

The woman's a blank. Scraped-back hair and a suit jacket, she's got her name badge wonky on a bit of string round her neck.

'Michael Burns. Got a half eleven appointment.'

'Take a seat. We'll shout you when we're ready.'

'It's half past now.'

'Take a seat.'

I do, and it's uncomfortable, a plastic primary school one. My phone buzzes. A text from Dig.

WEN U HOME. NEED BOGROLL.

The windows in the job centre overlook a staff car park. I don't know what the offices above this floor are used for but there are a lot of shiny cars with up-to-date plates out there. The rain's gone off but it sits on the windscreens like blisters and makes them all look diseased. A guy bounces into the waiting room, wearing a grey suit from a super-market and one leg of his pants tucked into his sock. He looks at everyone, right in the eyes if he can, and holds it till the other person looks away. When he gets to me I pretend like I never saw him come in and keep staring out the window. After a bit, a woman's voice calling my name makes me look round.

2

When I get out, it's gone one and it's started pissing down again so I jog round to the pub on the corner of the main road. The wooden benches on the concrete square outside are dripping and somebody's left a beer mat out on one that's turning to mush, next to a blue plastic ashtray that's a little dirty swimming pool. The glass panel in the front door's got a massive crack in it and it's been taped over a few times to hold it together. I push it carefully and step in then pull my hood down and walk across the lounge to the bar. It's dead quiet. I can hear a man's voice coming from the telly on the wall, something about someone signing for someone, and there's just a couple of old fellas in the corner, sitting there sipping smooth, not even talking, not even looking up. Pete, the landlord, is behind the bar, and I want to leave but he's seen me already.

'Sit down, Michael. Pint is it?'

'No, a half.'

I sit on a bar stool that has rips in the red leather cushion.

'Very funny.' His face is dead straight and he flicks the pump down and starts the lager pouring out. 'Must be dole day.'

'Yep.'

'And where's your man, Dick, is it?'

'Dig.'

'Right, Dig. Where's he?'

'Don't know.'

'He made a right fucking mess last time he was in here, Michael.' The pint pot is full, but he lets it run over a bit to get rid of some head. 'A right fucking to-do that was.'

'Yeah, Pete. I know.'

He sticks the glass down in front of me and wipes his hand on the arse of his jeans. One of the old fellas gets up from the corner and moves underneath the telly, close, like he's straining to see it.

'You're all right to come in here you know. You, but not him.'

Pete leans onto the bar and I can see some spilt beer soaking into the elbow of his shirt, but he doesn't notice or he doesn't care.

'Cheers, Pete.'

'Just make sure he's aware then, yeah?'

'Yeah, Pete.'

'That's two-ninety.'

I hand over the money and Pete puts it straight in his pocket. Then he turns round and opens the glass-washer to start emptying it. A big cloud of steam comes out and some of it lands on the mirrors on the back of the bar, blocking out my face.

The girl walks in. She looks round and comes straight over when she recognises me.

'All right?' Her hair is wet, a bit is stuck to her cheek like someone's drawn on her face with a brown pen while she was asleep. 'Get us a drink. I'm freezing.'

'What?'

'Vodka and tonic.' Her eyes are blue.

I order. Pete asks if she's old enough, then laughs and starts pouring anyway. When he puts it on the bar in front of her, I shift in my seat so it doesn't look like I don't want to talk.

'You saw me getting booted out of the dole before, didn't you?'

'Yeah. What did you do?'

'Fuck all. That fat bastard security guard just wanted a grip of me, I reckon.' She grins and her teeth are all white, then she takes a long swallow of her drink. 'I kicked off a bit. But only because they weren't listening to me.'

'Right,' I say because I think she's stopped, but she hasn't.

'Yeah. The fuckers. Make you feel dead small don't they, in there. I said, I'm not a just a number on your forms, you daft bitch.' She stands up. She is smaller now then when she was sat on the barstool. 'And I said, watch this, yeah, make sure this goes on the records, yeah?' She punches out her arm, quick. I think she probably gets some power behind it. 'Have this one as well.' Her skinny leg kicks out and knocks the side of the bar. Pete looks up from his paper. 'Then that security knob got me and I'm out of there, fast and skint as fuck.'

'Harsh.' I don't think it's harsh but I nod my head when I say it, then I see that I've finished my pint.

'Yeah, well harsh. Nice that someone gets it.' She goes

back to smiling and she looks at my empty glass. 'What you doing now?'

'Going home.'

'Where's that?'

'Old Trafford.'

'I'll come with you. Mine's round there.'

I sit for a minute and don't say anything. She keeps inspecting me, looking me up and down. When I get up and start walking to the door, she downs the rest of her drink and follows me. She walks quick like she needs to stay close to someone, taking fast little steps, and her head's down. I hold the door open behind me, for her. I can just see her mouth moving when she goes past but she's not saying anything out loud.

The rain holds off while we're walking to the tram stop. From the door of the pub, all the way back, she stays behind me, just a step. She speaks in short bursts. Like a machine gun.

'We paying or jumping it? Because I've not got any money. Don't matter, I suppose. I've had fines off it before. Have you? They don't really chase you for them. Can you hear that? Where's that coming from?'

My boots hit the pavement in a weird rhythm because I'm dodging snails that've come out in the wet. A guy walks towards us and he's got holes in his trainers and he's spraying something from a bottle onto his hand and rubbing it on his beard, then he tucks the bottle away, in the pocket of his dirty jacket. Then he does it again. When we go past him, it stinks of aftershave. I don't think she notices because she just carries on.

'Fucking hell, I'm starving. Let's get some food in a bit, yeah? Any takeaways near you? Got any cigs on you? Mike? Mike?' I feel a crunch under my foot but keep walking.

At the platform, I can't see any trams coming our way but there's a few people waiting so there must be one due. The lads who grinned at me in the dole are stood at the far end, looking over and one of them gives me this wave, dead floppy like his hand's going to come off, and his mate laughs, hard and long up at the sky.

'Who are they?' She's a little bird, turning her head up at me and squinting.

'No one.'

'Think they're taking the piss.'

'Let them.'

'Why?'

'Why not?'

'Because you don't have to.'

I don't know what she means so I just stare at the sign on the opposite platform that gives you the times of the last trams. I make myself look like I think it's dead interesting, even if it's too far away and I can't read it. We don't really say anything else until a tram pulls in. She presses the button for the doors and we get on and sit next next to each other, in the back half.

Lee – she tells me her name on the tram – likes to do loads of things. Mostly talk. I can see the bushes at the sides of

the track flying past in the wrong direction and it makes
me think for a minute that I'm falling into a big green hole,
so I have to quickly check behind me just to make sure
I'm not and steady myself. Her voice rolls along with the
noise in the carriage. If the wheels or the brakes or the air
going past outside goes a bit loud then I've lost what she's
saying half-way through and it takes me ages to get back to
understand what she's going on about again, she talks that
quick. Someone opens a window just as she turns to face
me, and she's curling one of her skinny legs underneath
herself and sitting on it.

'So, what do you reckon?'

I don't know what she's asking for.

'Come on. A night or two.'

I feel like I should ask her to ask me again. But I just say
'Yeah?' instead.

She smiles. A big smile of them white teeth, and I can
see some little red cracks in her bottom lip.

'Cheers, Michael. Saved my life, mate.'

She sits back properly and leans into me and puts her
head against my shoulder. It feels weird because there's
no weight to her. Just feels like my coat got heavier on me,
not like there's a person close up to me. She smells like the
wet concrete outside. There's no one in our carriage, but
there's four stops to go so maybe someone will get on and
see us sat here like this. Probably think we're some couple,
back from shopping, or going cinema in town. Sat together
and touching each other and happy. But I'm not. If I asked
Lee, I don't she'd be either. But she's asleep anyway.

3

Ten minutes' kip is all Lee gets. I think she's going to run when I nudge her to get her up for the stop. Her face goes like she's forgotten she's been talking all that shite to me for the last hour, like she doesn't know who I am. Then she smiles at me again and stands up to get off, like normal. We get up the ramp, off the platform, and start walking past the shops on the main road. She stops outside a takeaway called Pizza Magic and goes in her pocket for something. I want to keep walking to get home.

'Got a few quid, Michael?'

'Yeah.'

I give her some money and she ducks inside, and I follow her. The walls are orange and the paint's cracking in most places. Not like I haven't been in there before. Probably been too fucked to notice. She's already at the counter, on her tiptoes, and she's talking to the guy. He's foreign and he talks slow and quiet when he tells her how long her food is going to be. It's damp and the one big panel of glass on the shop front is steamed up. There are some plastic stools nailed to the floor next to a bit of a shelf that juts off the wall, like a shit bar because there's no drink, just a wall. I sit down, then Lee comes over and sits down too.

'I got you some chips,' she says.

'Cheers.' I'm not hungry.

She runs her hands across the tops of her legs where her jeans are wet from the rain. I don't know if she's waiting for me to say something more. Like buying chips that I don't really want with my own money needs a better answer.

'Where's yours from here?' She's flapping a menu about as a fan, round her face.

'Upstairs. We need to go round the back of the shops to get in.'

The fan thing she's doing is pissing me off because she's acting like it's hot in the takeaway, but it's not. It's just wet. Like it is outside. Water's been trod in on the lino floor, and there's some greasy wet marks on the counter top that I can just see without seeing exactly what they are. The wet on the big window's dripping onto the floor as well. The guy stood behind the counter, his hair is wet. Or greasy. Or maybe he's got too much of some kind of gel on it. It makes his head look like someone dunked a hedgehog in lube, and it's sitting up there like a hat.

'You want something too, mate?' the guy says.

'No. You're all right,' I say.

'The chips are for him,' Lee says to the guy.

'I'm not hungry,' I say to him.

'Yeah, you are.' She looks at me funny. 'I know you are. What have you ate today?'

'Nothing.'

'There you go then.'

She gets up, and stands by the counter with her back to me. I don't feel hungry, but my stomach is churning.

+

We go past three more takeaways on the walk round to the flat. At the end of the row of shops I turn right, down a half-alley. There's only buildings on one side. Just a low wall on the other. Over the wall it's the car park for the shops. Lee stays behind me like she has been doing, and she's struggling with a white plastic bag that's got two pizza boxes and some yellow cartons in it. At the end of the alley there's two concrete posts that we skirt round, and then we're in the car park, sort of, and I turn right and I can see a line of different-coloured skips, and the back entrances of all the takeaways and paper shops. There's shit all over the ground, mostly food wrappers, and I have to pretty much jump over some wet brown greasy stuff underneath the step of one of the back entrance doors. Lee swings her arm carrying the food before she jumps the puddle, like the weight of it might help her get over. There's a man I haven't seen before, leaning against a big silver minivan taxi and he's smoking. When he turns to face us he smiles and he almost looks like the guy who just served us in the takeaway, but older. I get to the door of the flat and wait for Lee. She catches up and I turn the key in the lock and let her in. Then I go in after her, and when I'm closing the door I catch another look at the smoking guy and he's still smoking, and he's staring right at me but he's not smiling any more.

'Michael?' Dig's voice bounces down at me.

'Yeah,' I say, but he probably can't hear that.

'Hello,' Lee shouts. We climb up, past a pile of letters on the stairs. I can hear the banister creaking each time Lee grabs at it. Dig is at the top now, and the light from the kitchen is bright behind him.

'All right?' he says, noticing Lee first, even though she is behind me. He is naked. Again. 'Brew?' he says. To her.

'Put some fucking clothes on,' I say as I go past him. Lee doesn't say anything back to him, and we all end up stood round the chest freezer in the kitchen like we're having a fucking meeting or something. I put my keys down on the side, bang them down, and look out the window and it's started raining again out there but the guy is still smoking outside his taxi and just standing in the rain. I can see him getting wet.

'What you got there?' Dig nods at the bag that Lee is still holding, even though she could put it down now.

'Pizza. Some chips. Fish fingers. Hot wings.' She's not still when she's saying it. Not all over the place. She's stepping from one foot to the next, just leaning her body, not a big fucking tap dance or anything.

'Fuck off, fish fingers?'

'Yeah.'

'From where?'

'Downstairs.'

'Bollocks.' He walks out.

'Do you want a drink, or something?' I say to her.

'No thanks. I just want to eat something.'

'Right. We can sit down upstairs.'

I walk out of the kitchen and hear the door downstairs slam. We – Lee is following me again – go upstairs again and the front room smells of cigs and Dig's computer is still on in the corner. There's a close-up picture of a girl's face on the screen. Her eyes are wet and there's make-up running down her face and her mouth is open. There's something behind her, over her shoulder, but the screen saver blinks on before I can see it. Lee has come past me because I am standing still in the doorway, just looking into the room instead of going into it. She sits on the red sofa in the corner and starts unpacking her food onto the round coffee table. She puts her pizza box on top of a magazine and flips the lid open. The smell makes me feel a bit sick, but she looks up then and I can tell she wants me to sit down with her. I do, and she fishes out a yellow carton and gives it to me.

'Chips,' she says.

The box is damp and it smells vinegary.

'I like it here.' Lee starts then and she picks up a tiny chicken wing with both hands and bites into it. I open my chips and pick one up, making an effort for her. I don't know why I do that. I can see Dig's screen saver moving, in the corner of my eye. I know what it says. It says, IM BORED.

'Anyway, so I lost my room in that house because of it and that's why I was at the dole booting off because I'm stressed out with it all, know what I mean, Mike?' Lee's white teeth have little specks of red on them from the pizza.

'Yeah. I know what you mean.'

'Yeah, so I was thinking I might be able to crash here for a bit? With yous.' She grabs a handful of the chips that I put back on the table and stuffs them into her mouth, and she's not looking at me.

'Depends what Dig says.'

'Fine,' Dig says over his shoulder, because he's back in the flat and back on his computer.

'Nice one. Cheers, Mike. Cheers, Dig.' Lee looks like she's going to stand up but she doesn't. She just shifts a bit and carries on eating. I ate some chips but not many, and Dig came back with some beer so I'm drinking one and Lee's drinking one, and Dig's drinking two. It's getting dark outside. It seems like I've been sat watching Lee eat all day. Dig turns round to us, sat on the sofa.

'We doing anything tonight? Town?'

'It's fucking Tuesday,' I say.

'Tuesday's the new Friday mate. Students are back.'

'Yeah, let's go out, Mike.' Lee stops eating and does look at me this time.

'Thought you were skint?'

'I am but, come on.'

Dig stands up and stretches his arms up over his head. 'Yeah, come on, Mike, you boring bastard.'

'Whatever. Fuck.'

4

The night's turned wild for some reason, gone windy and black, and it's dead cold. But it isn't raining any more. Lee said she would sleep on the floor later but I bet Dig tries to get into her. I don't know if she was telling the truth before, about losing her job, and losing her room. A waitress or something. The way she went at the takeaway though, she probably got sacked for eating everything. I can't get my hands warm so I jamb them in between my legs but they feel just as cold and thin. The tram rattles along and it's pretty empty, and I can only see one other person, who isn't us, the way I'm looking. A girl, stood up by the doors. She's got a pram, with shopping bags stuffed all underneath it, and I can't see the kid inside. Lee is chatting to Dig in the seats opposite, across the aisle. Her back is to me. Dig looks me in the eye, over her shoulder, and grins. She doesn't notice and keeps on talking.

My phone rings.

'All right, Mand.'

'Michael? Where are you?' She's out of breath.

'Just going into town with Dig.'

'Right. I've just got out of work. I'll meet you somewhere. I'll text you when I'm leaving the house.'

'OK.'

'Do you need some money tonight?'

'No. It's fine. See you later.'

'All right. I'll bring you some. See you later.'

She waits on the end until I hang up.

The stairs down to the bar are narrow and the bulbs on the cracked walls are lit up old and yellow. The air coming up is warm, and I start feeling like it might not be so bad, coming out on a Tuesday, with a mate and some bird, for a few, and your sister's coming too and she'll buy a couple, and it's seems like a pretty good idea all of a sudden and when I actually step up to the bar to order I'm smiling. The guy behind the bar looks too young to be serving drinks, but he sorts ours out quickly and we all turn around and start looking for a free table. Something like Joy Division is playing on the jukebox, but it sounds too loud and too clean, and I'm glad when Dig spots a few chairs in the corner and we move out of the middle of the room. We sit for a bit, and don't really talk much. Lee looks at me over the top of her glass while she has a sip of her drink, then she smiles. Dig doesn't sit still at all. He takes swigs of his pint and leans backwards and forwards and to each side in his chair if any girl walks near the table. After a while, I think that it doesn't even matter what they look like or how they're dressed. Just that they're there. In front of him. It makes me feel like saying something to him, but I don't know how, and I don't know what.

We drink for an hour, pretty much. Dig gets up to put some tunes on at one point but other than that we all just sit there and drink, fast. Lee talks most of the time, keeping something flowing between us all, and she's sat on the middle of the three chairs so her head turns left and right between me and Dig. Dig and me drink some beer that comes in a tall pint glass, and Lee keeps having vodka and tonic, being stingy with the tonic so it stretches across a few lots of vodka. When Mand walks over to us, I realise there isn't a chair for her so I stand up.

'Hey.' She gives me a hug and sits down and she smells really nice. She's got a vodka and coke, I think.

'Hiya.' I lean on the end of the bar next to the table. 'That was quick.'

'Really felt like a drink tonight. Couldn't be bothered pissing around at home for ages.' She takes a big swallow, and scans the room. 'Few people about, isn't there?'

'Yeah. Dig reckons it's always busy now the students are back.' I look over at him. He doesn't say anything. I don't think he has looked over since Mand came in. He doesn't speak to her because one time she told him to fuck off. She doesn't speak to him because she thinks he's a knob.

'Hiya,' Mand says and she leans over to Lee. 'I'm Michael's sister. Amanda.'

'Oh, hiya.' Lee smiles a big smile. 'I'm Lee. I'm just staying with Mike and Dig for a bit. In the flat. On the floor.' Lee finishes her drink and then she does a little look down and for the first time I see her look a bit awkward. 'Just going toilet. I'll get some drinks on the way back.'

Mand has been chatting for a bit now, about how shit work is and how there's another guy trying it on in there with her. Someone's turned the music up in the bar so we're talking close into each other's ears. She says something about a warehouse environment, with no daylight, regimented break times, and restricted areas, gives you a sort of prison effect. When I say that's probably why all the blokes keep trying it on with her she just gives me a dig but laughs a bit. She's in a good mood tonight. Sometimes I see her and she can't move. I had to break into her flat once because when I went round to see her the door was locked but when I went to the living room window I could just see her through a gap in the curtains, lying on her side, on the floor. I remember her eyes were open because I thought she was dead at first, but when I got in I could hear her breathing like normal, only she wasn't there. I had to just lift her up off the floor and put her on the couch and I didn't have a clue what to do except just sit there, me staring at her open eyes and she didn't blink once. In the end, I went out to make a brew and I think she heard the kettle boiling from wherever she was because she shouted through that she'd have one too , and I fucking shat myself because it'd been so quiet.

'Where are you, Michael?' Mand says in my ear, over the music.

'What do you mean?' I'm still sitting next to her and I'm holding an empty pint pot with both hands and looking hard into it. 'I'm here, aren't I? Getting wrecked.'

The club is packed. Dig wasn't wrong. Bodies everywhere. More drink on the floor than in people's glasses or guts. Lee and me are in a corner near a black column that has a shelf where you can put your drink down, but the shelf is covered in empties so we hold our bottles against our chests while we half-talk. I can feel myself doing the usual. Trying hard to act sober. Rolling inside and wishing I was anywhere but down in that dark, sweaty mess. Imagining how good it'll be when we leave and the air is cold again. Lee leans into me to speak, but I brush her off a bit because I know the sound of her voice will make me feel sick. She tries again.

'Do you feel different?' She takes a swig from the bottle of blue shit she's drinking.

'Yeah. I'm bollocksed.'

'No. All the time.'

'Most of the time.' That makes me laugh and I try to smile at a girl as she walks past but she doesn't see me, and I put the bottle in my right hand up to my mouth to have a drink but it's empty so I drop it on the floor. The glass goes everywhere, silently.

'Not pissed up, you knob. Different *inside*.'

'Are you trying to send me under?' She's wrecked. Must be. Talking shite. I start moving away a bit, like I want the toilet, or the bar.

'Michael.' She moves after me and grabs my arm with her bony little hand. 'Michael. I know what it's like. I know, Michael.'

I go to the toilets and puke in a urinal while three guys watch.

Mand comes up to me at the bar and when she sees the dark patch on my T-shirt and the sick on my trainers she gets our coats. One of the bouncers on the door says something to his mate, about me, when we go past. We wait in a doorway over the road while Dig tries to flag a taxi, because it's raining again. Lee and Mand are talking quietly and I lean out from under the black archway and let the water hit the back of my head. After a while it starts to run around my neck and drip off my chin. I watch the drops fall a few times then start to feel sick again so I try to get in on the conversation to distract myself.

'I know what you mean,' Mand is saying. 'Just being able to walk away, make a break for it, sort of thing?'

'Yeah, it's great. No ties, no nothing. Sometimes I don't even know what I'm doing on that day.' Lee is nodding her head when she says this, like she's agreeing with herself.

'Fucking scary,' I say.

'Shut up, Michael. Who asked your pisshead opinion?' Mand folds her arms and looks at me.

'No one.'

'Exactly.'

Lee lights a cigarette. 'Don't you want to be free, Mike? Do you believe in freedom?'

'What?'

'Freedom, Michael?' Mand says. 'Do what you want, when you want?'

I look out at the road, at a parked black cab. A girl is climbing into the back seat on all fours. Her dress is up round her hips, so her arse is hanging out. She's got one shoe on and her bare foot is dirty. I take the lit cigarette out of Lee's mouth and take a drag myself. I say, 'Why would I want that?' and I blow the smoke out into the night.

5

'You set, mate?' Dig leans forward when he says it, so it's quiet and in my ear. The black cab is close to the flat now, and the meter is blinking up quickly to nearly twelve quid. Fuck that. I'm set. My hand is on the door handle, just gentle, resting there, not even thinking of doing a runner. I look over at Mand and she's doing the same on her side. If I could look behind me I reckon the driver's eyes would be flicking from the road to us to the road to us to us and back to the road, knowing what we're about before it's happened.

'Just here near the bus stop, mate,' Dig says. He even goes into his pocket like he's getting his money ready. 'Cheers, pal. Nice one.' The cab brakes and stops and when I look up and along the windows of the flats I can see a light we left on.

No one says anything. When the doors click open, nearly at the same time, we're gone. Straight for the alley, and for the dark car park, then try to get into the flat before the driver can even realise he was right and that he never should've picked us scrotes up. Mand is less pissed and she's up ahead. I can see her hair flapping on her back as she sprints. I hold back behind Dig, because he's got the keys and they're jingling in his hand and when he heads down the alley and I can't see him for a few seconds, I follow the sound. When I come out of the dark, I have a quick look back for Lee. She's not there. I hear the back gate swing open once, then again, and the keys going into the lock of the door. Mand and Dig, in. I scrape the bottom of my shoe on the ground because it feels like I've stepped in something. The alley is still dark. I want her to come flying out. Bump into me. Scared, and I have to put an arm round her and run her to the flat because she doesn't really know which one it is. She's only been once. I start to walk slowly back up the alley to the road.

Lee is struggling, hard. Like at the job centre but her anger's not there and she's not shouting the odds. Her face is screwed up ugly. The driver's got her arm, a proper tight hold and he's a pretty big guy, and I think he's trying to put her back in the taxi. He's shouting.

'Bitch! Little bitch!' Spitting it everywhere.

Lee unzips her coat and pulls her arm out of the sleeve but she does it too quick and she pulls away but she dumps herself on the floor, on her shoulder. I think a bit of her head bounces on the road too. She makes a noise like a hiss. The driver puts her coat on the top of the car. I wait for Lee to get up. If she gets up now I can shout so she knows where I am and we can just do one round to the flat. She doesn't get up quick though. She doesn't see me. The driver kicks her in the stomach. Then he gets back in the taxi and drives off, fast. Lee's coat falls off the back a bit away.

I start walking over after I see the taxi turn right at the

lights at the top of the road. Lee stays down, not really moving, just breathing heavy. I can see one of her hands is tangled up in her hair.

'Lee?'

She looks up at me and there's a bit of red on her lip, that looks wet in the street light.

'Mike. Hey. Sorry. I didn't know we were running.' She takes her hand down from the side of her head. Her hair comes with it and stands out like straw.

'Do you want a lift up?'

'Thanks.'

Lee's wrist is small in my hand, and when she gets on her feet I know that she's not right because she holds onto my shoulder. I'm standing in the road, head down, and she's standing next to me, head down, looking like we're talking about something serious. If anyone was watching. I look up at the flat window and the light's still on but I can't see anyone moving about.

'My head hurts, Mike.'

I don't look at her. 'Oh. It'll be OK. Do you want to go up?'

'Can we not? I want to stay out here for a bit.' She let's go of me and walks over to the kerb.

'Come and sit here.' She sits down, and stretches her legs into the road. It's dead quiet. I walk over. I scrape my shoes when I walk. I don't sit down. She is messing with the side of her head again, pushing on it with one finger, then the palm of her hand, and checking, probably for blood.

'Sit down.'

'I'm all right.'

'Sit down, Mike.'

I look up and down the road, like I'm checking for someone coming. Then I look up at the flat again. Nobody is looking back. Nobody is looking at us. I zip up my coat to the top. I sit down next to her.

'Good night, yeah? Sorry about this.'

'It's all right. Doesn't matter, does it?'

'I just mean, I should've read you better. Should've known you were going to do a runner.' She sniffs. I hear her swallow afterwards.

'You'll know next time. We always fucking do it.'

'Yeah. Yeah. Am I bleeding?' She puts the side of her head near my face. There is a little wet patch in her hair.

'A bit. Nothing's coming out. It's stopped already.'

'Mike?' She faces me.

'What?'

'Are you tired?'

'Yeah.'

'We can go upstairs now.'

I stand up and put my hands in my pockets. 'OK.'

'Mike?'

I don't say anything. I start walking. I go slowly at first, then I speed up when I hear her get up.

The stairway is dark but I know where most of the shit is so I don't trip. I think Lee just keeps her eyes on my back. It feels that way. She's staring at me while we go up. At the top, I go into the kitchen and she follows me. I fill the kettle up to the top and put it on. She's still staring at me.

'Lee. What?'

I can see her eyes getting wet. They're so blue it looks like they're freezing.

'You hate this, don't you? Don't you, Mike? You fucking hate this!' She runs out. The door bangs shut. She trips once on the way up the second set of stairs, to the front room. I don't hear the top door slam. The kettle boils loud then clicks off. I don't make a drink. I sit on the chest freezer and look out of the window. I can mostly just see myself reflected back.

In the front room the electric heater is on and it smells like burning dust. The light is on. Dig is asleep on the bed. Mand is lying on the couch. I don't know if she's asleep, or pretending to be. Lee is sitting on the floor by the TV. It's on a channel I don't know, and the volume is off. I sit down behind Lee, on the armchair.

'Are you all right?'

'I'm fine. I was sad. Sorry.' She spins and looks up. There are lines down her cheeks.

'I need to go somewhere tomorrow,' she says, quietly.

'Where?'

'To my uncle's. I need to get some money. You doing anything?'

'No.'

'Come with me.'

'OK.' I check my phone. It's gone four. 'Look. I want my bed. Do you want me to sort you out some stuff to sleep?'

'No, I'll stay up.'

'Do you want anything?'

'No, thanks.'

I don't want to move Mand, even if she isn't asleep yet, so I just cross my arms over me and put my head back on the chair. Lee gets up and turns off the light. I see her shadow on the cracked ceiling as she moves back in front of the telly and sits down. She shuffles back and leans up against the chair I'm on, between my legs.

6

'Up up up, fuckers.' Dig is singsong-shouting. 'Up up up.'
Like someone's Mum. The window is propped open and
cold air is getting in at the bottom of my jeans. My neck is
stiff. Lee is stood over by the window, looking down at the
road. Mand has gone to work already. I try to say something
to Lee but it comes out like shit.

'Brew? Anyone?'

'Please. Thanks, Dig.' Lee doesn't turn from the window
but she smiles when she's finished talking. I just nod my
head, then hold it in my hands because it feels like it'll fall
off if I don't.

Dig's gone somewhere. Lee is talking about a guy from last
night. I am watching the TV, hard. Her voice is making me
feel sick.

Then she says, 'Shall we go then?'

'To your uncle's?'

'Yeah. Just need to jump the tram back into town. He's
near the arena.'

'Right.'

She puts her coat on. It's dirty up the back. I stick my
hand out to brush at it, but she's already moving to the

door and my hand just falls down by my side. I put my coat on and get my hat out of the inside pocket and pull that on. In the mirror by the door I can see the hat looks wonky but I leave it and pull my hood up as well. I can hear Lee on the toilet downstairs and I listen and when she's finished I go downstairs.

The walk and tram ride make me sweaty. I feel like crying. I remember a time when I came home fucked once and Mand stood there shouting at me while I sat down and then lay down in the hallway and I didn't bother to close the door behind me. Rain came in and a dog outside stood on the pavement looking in like it wanted to come out of the rain. I remember crying then because I just wanted the inside of me to stop for a minute so I could breathe. I can feel that sort of shit now. Lee might bring it on. She is staring out of the window as we rush past people rushing across Piccadilly Gardens. I see a woman pulling a suitcase behind her that is some fucking rotten pink colour. Then I look back at the grey floor of the tram.

'You rough, Mike?'

'Huh?'

'Not far now. Want me to open a window?' She gets up.

'Whatever. Yeah. Cheers.'

She sits back down. 'Ian owns 7th Heaven.'

'Who's Ian?' I cough out.

'My uncle.'

'What's 7th Heaven?'

'A massage place.'

I wait a bit, in case there's more. I'm fucking sick of talking. She's looking out of the window again.

'Do you work there?'

'No, I fucking don't.'

On Swan Street, one side of the pavement is blocked off with builders' fences. We walk along in the gutter next to the fences, then cross over when there's a gap in the cars. We go past a silver office building with an orange sign that isn't written in English. On the bit of pavement in front there are three trees; two of them have leaves and the other one doesn't. It doesn't look like a tree, next to the other two. I stop. Lee stops.

'What?' she says.

On the right of the bare tree, there are two stumps sticking out of the ground where other trees have been cut down.

'It's give up,' I say.

'What?' she says.

'That tree's give up.' I point at the tree with no leaves. 'His mates are fucked.' I point at the two stumps. 'He knows what's coming.'

I start walking again, and she does the same. There is a gap in the buildings, a gap in between the office block and the row with 7th Heaven on. Like something has moved away, like the building that was there just went. Or the office has shuffled along a bit because it doesn't want to touch the club. There is a no-parking sign on the wall of the gap. No one has parked there. The front of the building is white and there's a blue shop shutter rolled down and a blue and white door, open, on the right. There is a blue sign sticking out over the pavement and a yellow and blue sign over the door and they both say 7th Heaven. There are two bin bags outside. A big black one and a small white one. Lee goes through the blue and white door.

The stairway is tight and some of the bulbs in the lights are blown. The carpet looks blue. There's no noise coming from in front; I can just hear the cars getting quieter outside as we go up. About ten steps and Lee stops quickly. I look up over her shoulder and I can see a camera with a blinking red dot eye set up in the corner between the wall and the ceiling, next to a door, which is shut. The door is heavy-looking. We stand there, not doing anything. Lee is looking up into the camera. Then a big man opens the door.

'Yeah?'

'Hiya,' Lee says.

'We don't have any work, darling.' He laughs.

'Just let us in, yeah?'

'What's it about?'

'Just let us in, for fuckssake.'

He stands there, like he might recognise her, confused. Then he looks at me. Then he shuts he door. We stand there, not speaking. I feel less sick, but I sit on one of the steps anyway with my back to the door. A guy starts coming up the stairs and he's not looked up yet. I think he sees my shoes first, then me sat down, then Lee, when she turns round.

'Jesus-fucking-Christ.' He says it quick under his breath, then he goes back down the stairs and out. Pretending like he came in for directions, I reckon. Lee laughs and the door opens. The big man is there again. He is smiling.

'Lee, sweet. Come in.'

I walk past a desk with an open notepad on it. The page is covered in writing, I try to read a bit but Lee is moving fast. Down a corridor, past an open door with a guy sat watching the news on a small TV, then past a few closed doors, then through a door at the end and into another corridor with two more doors, one closed, one open. Lee knocks on the closed door. I try to look in through the open door but it's dark inside. No one says anything after the knock then Lee turns the handle and goes in. There's a guy inside, talking on the phone, but he puts it down when he sees us.

'Lee.' He stands up and he smiles.

'Ian,' Lee says and she holds her hand out. He grabs it and holds it when he looks at me.

'Michael,' I say.

'Michael,' he says, and he smiles and he lets go of Lee's hand. 'Good to meet you, lad.' He's got a grey shirt on.

Lee closes the door. 'Are you OK, Ian? How's Chris?'

'She's all right, Lee. I'm fine. You all right?'

'Good, yeah.'

The room is small and there is paper piled up on the desk that Ian is stood behind. The window behind him is blacked out. Someone has left a mug on the window ledge.

'So. What you two doing here, sweet?' He sits down again.

'Just seeing how you are, Ian. I like fussing, don't I?'

'And?'

'To see if you might have anything spare?'

He's already going in his back pocket and she hasn't finished speaking. He puts a roll of notes on the desk.

'Yours,' he says, not looking at me.

'Ian, I don't just come for that, you know. Honest.' She doesn't look embarrassed. 'Honest, I like checking on you.'

'I'm glad, sweet. I'm glad. Any time you need though, yeah?' He puts his elbows on the desk in front of him and puts his fists together and puts his chin on his fists.

'Do you need anything else?'

'Not right now.' Lee says that quickly. And she has a quick look at me.

'I won't see you go without, sweet. Any time, yeah?'

'Yeah, Ian. Thanks.'

We go back out the door and Ian goes back on the phone.

We go back down the corridor. The bloke watching TV has gone, and there's no one between us coming out of the office and walking back to the front desk. The big guy isn't waiting for us. I go to open the heavy door.

'Lee! Lee! Turn round, you fucking tart!'

It makes me jump. The girl's voice is loud as fuck and it's been dead quiet in the place. I turn round. Lee is hugging the other girl. She's taller and looks older. She's got a bikini on.

'Alex, hiya. I didn't even know you were on today.' Lee stands back and I can see that the girl has got a tattoo of a gun at the top of her leg. 'Are you OK?'

'Same as always, gorgeous. On me back for crack. You know it, little Lee. What's going on with you? You look great.' The other girl puts her hands on Lee's shoulders and looks like she's studying her. 'Looking a proper lady, eh?'

'Shut up, Alex. Whatever.'

'Serious. Looking gorgeous.' The girl flicks her hair at me. 'This your new boy?'

'No.' I don't know if Lee says it, or I say it, or we both say it. The girl laughs and folds her arms under her tits and looks at me.

'Shame. Does he want business?'

'No.' Lee says that.

The girl, Alex, takes us to the room with the TV in. I make sure I don't sit where that guy was sat before.

'Look, where you staying? You all right somewhere?' she says to Lee.

'I'm staying with Mike at the moment. Not far. Old Trafford.' Lee is smiling. Alex makes her smile, I think.

'Good. Good. That's all right then. Have you got money? Seen Ian?'

'Yeah, saw him. He sorted me out. It's all right, Alex. You don't have to keep worrying, you know.'

'But I will anyway. Little Lee. Got to look out for little Lee. Give us your number. Lost me old phone.'

They both get their phones, and Lee reads her number out loud for Alex to type in. I try not to listen. The TV's still got the news on. Someone is missing and they keep replaying clips of an old couple crying, and there's a police logo on the wall behind their heads while they cry. Lee stands up.

'Just going for a piss.' She goes out. The TV is on mute. It is quiet.

'So, Mikey. You all right?' the girl, Alex, says to me.

'Fine. Cheers.'

She leans in a bit.

'Look,' she says, 'come back any time, yeah. On your own. I'll knock you a bit off. For looking after my little Lee.' She smiles.

'Yeah,' I say, like I agree.

The old woman on the TV has got snot all on her top lip and it stops me getting a hard-on.

Outside, it's getting dark already. We walk back up to the Gardens and go in the Piccadilly for a drink. Lee's round, she says. It's just filling up a bit with people coming out of work. The barmaid looks pissed off when I say that I want a pint. We stand in the corner, even though there are still seats about. Lee holds her bottle with both hands.

'Thanks for coming with me, Mike.'

'It's all right.'

'Why don't you text Dig. And Mand. Get them to come here.'

'Yeah. OK.'

7

Wrecked again. All of us, wrecked. Don't know the time.
Mand's dancing with some old fella in the corner to whatever shit is on the jukebox. I can't even hear it. Always got
to drink more the second night, to get where you were. My
guts feel wet. All liquid. Dig's got his head on the bar. He
was talking to the pissed-off barmaid before but she moved
to the other end of the bar and he just stayed were he was
sat, with his head getting lower each time he had a shot.
Lee is lying down in one of the booths on the far wall. Her
legs are sticking out and her trainers aren't touching the
floor. The wall on my back is keeping me up. I want to go
outside and get some air. The carpet looks like sick. The
rubber mats at the door are plain black, good to stand on.
I get there and put my empty glass on the floor slowly so
it doesn't break. Then I grab the gold handle on the door
and it pulls open easy even though it looked too heavy, so
I sort of jump outside quickly before the door shuts again.
In case it traps me that time. In case it gets heavy. Fuck.
The lights around the Gardens are stretched out like mad.
It's cold, and I feel sick because of the cold in the air. Fresh
air. I start walking.

One foot. Next foot. Head down. A guy goes past and says something like, 'You gay there, mate?'

I say back fast, 'Youfuckingwhat?' then turn around but I can't see him any more and I'm outside a bank on Market Street, and the blue in its sign is too bright. I get some money out of the machine. I keep going til the end of the Arndale and turn right and walk up to the Wheel. Some more people walk past and I walk towards them a bit when they get near me, so they have to walk on the road to let me go past, and they don't say anything to me. There are more of them, dressed up now, birds looking nice and lads milling around for a cig and a fight. I keep going past and up the hill to cross the tram lines and I can nearly see back to the Gardens on my right when I'm crossing the road, but it's the walk that I need. A big circle of air. And for all these fuckers to keep away while I walk. I bang shoulders with a guy who has got a girl with him and he says sorry to me. I want to have a girl walking with me. I keep walking, faster now, up away from the tram lines and past the bus station. The smell from a takeaway makes me hungry, and I start running.

I make it back. I look at the two proper trees and the one with no leaves. The two stumps next to it. I go over the the first stump and put my hand on it. There is a scratch in one side, like someone's put a knife into it, and a bit of hard bird shit that starts on the top and drips off the edge. I go over to the next stump and touch that, then move over and stand in front of the bare tree. I want to say something, out loud. I turn around and put my arse on it and my hands on my knees. An engine starts on my right and someone pulls their car out of the no-parking gap at the side of 7th Heaven. The silver van rolls backwards into the road and keeps coming back until the driver's window is right in front of where I'm leaning. I can't see who's inside. It sits there for a few seconds then drives off too slowly. I watch it go. Then stand up and turn to the doorway. The sign that sticks out over the pavement is lit up. It's colder now than it was before.

The staircase is still dark. I keep looking up at the heavy door at the top; each step up and it gets bigger. I try not to look at the camera on the wall. I wonder if the big guy is on the other side, watching me come up. I wonder if he's waiting to open the door for me and say hello and be friendly. I get to the top step and the heavy door stays shut, so I knock. I hear someone move on the other side and hear a bolt slide back and the door opens and the big guy is there again. He doesn't say anything. I step up and go inside and he closes the door after me then walks over to the front desk and into a door behind it. There is a girl sat at the desk. She looks older than Lee, but still young. She is wearing glasses and she has a mug next to her and I can smell coffee. The girl is looking at me. I look at her. She has a pen in her hand and she taps it on the desk.

'Did you ring?' she says.

'No,' I say.

'Fifty.' She puts her hand out. I get it out and pass it to her. She counts it and puts it in a tin and puts the tin under the desk.

'Right. Do you want to leave your coat?' she says.

'No.'

'Drink?'

'No.'

'Right. The lounge is just through that door. Sit down. The girls will come to you.'

'Alex,' I say.

'Right,' she says, 'Just go and sit down, yeah?'

She looks different, when she comes in. She's wearing black boots instead of trainers.

'Mikey! All right, darling.' She sits down on the sofa next to me. 'Someone said you wanted to see me.' She smiles. 'Does Lee know you've come back?' she says quietly.

'No.' My tongue feels fat in my mouth. The newsreader on the TV has a red tie.

'So. What you after, sweet?' She leans forward a bit. 'You want to come with me, don't you?'

'OK.'

I stand up with her, and she gets hold of my hand and takes me out of the TV room and down the corridor. We go past a couple of shut doors and then into another room. There's something that looks like a hospital trolley on one wall, but it's got no wheels. It's got a padded black mat on it. She walks me over to it then drops my hand and goes back to shut the door. There is a shower cubicle in the corner. I step sideways a bit when she walks back over to me and I knock into a table that's next to the trolley with my leg. It's got a load of johnnies on it and some baby wipes and some baby oil. The label for the oil isn't on the bottle. It's stuck flat on the edge of the table and I can see a long black hair stuck to it as well because it's see-through plastic.

'Now, why don't you just get your stuff off and jump up on there? I'll give you a massage.'

She puts one hand on my shoulder and her other hand starts undoing my belt. I let her do it and then I get my jeans and boxers off and sit up on the trolley. She unzips my coat and drops it on the floor and pulls my top over my head.

'On your front, sweet.'

I lie on my front on the trolley and it smells like perfume mixed with something else. The plastic is cold on my cheek. I close my eyes. I hear a squirting noise. She puts her hands on the top of my back and starts to rub across my shoulders. Some music starts, and a guy keeps talking over the tune that's being played so that I can't tell if it's decent or not because he's talking so much it's covering up the music and it starts to piss me off and I wish the guy would shut the fuck up and I want to get up and smash the radio into the floor and then one of her hands slides down my arse cheek and onto my balls and I don't give a shit about the guy on the radio any more.

The door swings open and a naked old guy falls through and lands on my coat. The girl stops what she's doing and climbs off the trolley and shouts out something and I sit up. The guy's making a sound like a plughole that's blocked, like the water's only going down slowly. He's got his face down but I can see his hands are around his neck.

'Get out! Get out!' the girl, Alex, starts shouting, 'Ray! Ray! Ian!'

The guy looks up then and he's confused but he's still strangling himself. I start to get down off the trolley to get dressed. Something wet hits the top of my foot when I stand up. I look down and there is a line of red across it, thin like a paper cut. The old guy makes the sound again but a bit louder. The girl runs out. I'm looking at the guy and he takes one hand off his neck and tries to touch my leg. He's looking up at me and I can't stop looking at his watery eyes even though he's naked too and he has shit-loads of black spots across his back and folds in the skin under his arms. Then both my feet go warm and when I look at them they're covered in red and there's red all over the floor, pouring out of the guy from underneath his hand and down his chest and flooding out round him. He puts both of his hands down on the floor and it looks like he's puking up the blood for a minute until he falls into it and stops making the sound and stops moving altogether. I sit back down on the trolley because all of my clothes are covered in red and I just stare at the red patch on the carpet as it gets bigger and I think it looks better than anything I've ever seen. I don't even notice the big guy from the door coming in and stepping over the old guy on the floor. He hits me hard with something that I don't see.

8

There's a girl with blood smeared all over her face and a guy sat laughing in the corner. It looks like the girl's crying at first but she's not, she's laughing as well and some red blood drips off her chin and onto the blue carpet and turns black. She rubs her hands across the floor and lifts them up to look and they come up bright red, and she laughs harder. There's something black stuck in her teeth. The guy's rocking back on his chair and he's killing himself laughing, looking at the girl on the floor and then looking at the ceiling and roaring his fucking head off. It's so loud. There's something on the floor next to where the girl is kneeling, next to where her legs are tucked under her, next to her black boots. It looks like a pile of clothes. The girl sticks her hand inside the pile and moves it around. She comes out with a tie that's covered in red and she crawls across the floor on her knees towards the guy. She does it like it's sexy or something. Then she kneels up and flicks up the collar on the guy's shirt and then does the tie up around his neck dead slow. She sits back and laughs more and spits something into the air, and he laughs and slaps his legs and stamps his feet.

+

I open my eyes and someone's walking over to me. I can see their shoes stepping on the blue carpet, getting closer, but I can't turn my head up to look at their face because my neck is stiff as fuck. When I touch it it hurts.

'Come on, Michael. Get up.' It's a man's voice. I think it's Ian. 'Get up.'

I can't move properly. He grabs me around the arms and pulls and I try to make my legs work and stand up and look at him. I try to say something.

'Don't worry, Michael. This way, yeah?' he says, and he starts leading me out of the room. The empty room. We go down the corridor back to the front desk. All the doors on either side are open and when we go into the TV room, the TV is off.

'Sit down.'

I sit down in the same seat I was in before. I've got clothes on. I don't know where my coat is.

'How's your head?'

'Great.'

'Good. Look. Sorry about that.' He sits down. 'That old fella was trying to get a bit rough with one of the new girls. She panicked.' He looks down. 'I don't even know why I'm explaining this to you.'

'Me either. I don't give a fuck. I want to go.' I put my hand up to the back of my head and it feels sticky there. 'I'm going,' I say and I stand up. He stands up quickly.

'Look, Michael. Because you came in here with Lee,

yeah? Because you were all right with her. You know what I'm going to say, don't you?'

'I'm going.' I start towards the front desk and the heavy door. He shouts after me.

'Say nothing, Michael. Quiet as the night, yeah?'

I don't look back or say anything. I pull the door open and get down the stairs. I'm outside and up the road a bit before I realise it's getting light.

Mand's front room light is on when I get there because she's up for work. I try the door to see if it's open but it isn't so I knock. I see her ghost through the glass as she comes over.

'What the fuck do you want?' She sort of smiles but I can tell she's pissed off and tired as fuck. I just walk in past her and go to the kitchen and put the kettle on.

'Oi. I've got work, you know.'

'I know. Sorry.'

She stands there looking at me with her arms crossed. Like Mam.

'I'm sorry, yeah? Can I just stay here for a bit today?'

'Right. Don't fuck anything up.' She walks up the stairs. 'Don't get Dig round.' She's not talking loud but she makes sure I hear that.

I make two brews and leave one on the side for her. Then I lie down on the couch in the front room and start drinking mine slowly. It feels good to lie down. Something shifts on the floor next to me. I reach up over my head and put the brew down then turn on my side. The old guy's looking up at me from the floor. He's lying on Mand's carpet and the red is spreading out all around him like a flower. I look up at the ceiling and then back down and the old guy's gone but the red is still there and it looks like a puddle. It's deep as if there's a hole in the floor. The surface of it moves like there's wind. Or something in it. I get down off the couch and stand next to it. The surface moves again. I kneel down and I blink and I end up on the floor looking at nothing and Mand is stood at the door. I can still smell something though.

'You all right?'

'Yeah. Yeah.' I get up and lean over to pick up my drink. She sees my head.

'What the fuck is that? What did you do?'

'Oh. I fell last night. Wrecked outside the pub. Just went home cause I didn't want to come back in looking like a cunt with blood all over me. It's fine.'

'It better be. Stay here til I get back from work. We'll talk.'

My phone rings in my pocket and wakes me up. I don't know the number.

'Yeah?'

'Mike. Michael. Hiya.' It's Lee.

'All right.'

'Where are you?'

'At Mand's.'

'Right.'

I wait for her to carry on.

'Right. Just seeing if you were all right. Where did you go last night?'

'Nowhere. Home.'

'But you're at Mand's now?'

'Yeah.'

'OK. OK. I'm just in town.'

'Right.'

'Right. So. Speak to you later, yeah?'

'Yeah.'

I put the phone down and get off the couch. There are sharks on the TV. And a diver in a cage. I go upstairs for a piss.

Later, I press the microwave start button and walk back into the front room. I didn't hear my phone go off again but there's a picture message on the screen when I check it. I open it. There's no message and I don't know the number. It's a picture of a red tie, lying on a desk.

'Ah fuck off.'

I say it out loud. The microwave pings. I go through and take the soup out. It's hot but I eat it quickly with some bread out of Mand's cupboard and dump the bowl in the sink. I go back to the couch but I turn my phone off before I lie down again.

A girl is pointing a gun at me only it's not a real gun it's a cartoon and it's flicking in and out of focus in her hands. She's naked. The room is dark but there is a light behind her coming from a doorway. She turns a bit and flicks the gun from me to the doorway. I start walking. She lets me go past, then I know she's following and keeping me going. It's cold. I'm naked. The light is bright but it doesn't hurt my eyes even though I've been in the dark room. I can smell something. I step through the doorway and I can see a man sat in a chair, with his back to me. He is naked. His back is old and there are black spots on it. He is looking at the floor. There is a pool of red around him. I walk up behind him and stop and look back at the girl with the gun. She nods. I put my hands around the old guy's neck and under his chin and start to twist and his head comes off in my hands. I turn it round to look at his face but he doesn't have one, it just keeps turning and his hair and the back of his neck go on forever. I throw the head away. The body starts to shake and the old hands grip the sides of the chair. Red leaks from the hole in the neck. The body shakes more. The red flows faster. The girl starts to laugh. I can smell something beautiful. I look down and I am covered in red.

9

I tell Lee I'll meet her in the pub. It's round the corner from
Mand's and I don't even know if Lee will know where. She
never asked. The door swings closed behind me but a few
steps up the road I can still hear the shit that Mand's got
on the TV. My head's banging and a few beers probably
won't help but Lee rang a few times mithering so in the
end it's easier to have a headache. The cold feels good
and it's not raining out. I get to the chicken place on the
corner and skirt left round the back of the dry cleaners
and across another road and through the side door of the
pub. It's busy. A group of lads at the pool table are shouting
about something and they're all laughing and holding onto
the edge of the table like they're going to fall over it's that
funny. I see Lee sat up at the bar looking at her phone so
I go over. She puts her phone away quickly when she sees
me and orders me a pint.

'Ray did that? Why?' she says, I think because she saw
the back of my head when she came back over from the
toilet. Her face has gone a bit red from the drink and the
pub is quieter now.

'Fuck knows.' I pull my hood half up to cover whatever's
there.

'Why did you go back? Was it Alex?' She sounds different when she says that. 'Did Alex get you to go back?'

'No. No. I was wrecked, yeah? I just went back.' My pint is done and I want another.

'But you went back?'

'Yeah.'

'To fuck something?'

'What?' I look down at my hands holding the empty glass and I roll it against my leg. 'Yeah. Probably.'

'Are you sure?' She says that differently as well. 'Did you think that? When you were walking?'

I look at her and her big blue eyes looking at me. She just stares until I speak.

'I don't fucking know. I don't know.'

'So you don't know why you went back, really.' She says it like she's won a competition, and she smiles. 'Do you want another drink?'

'Christ. Do I?'

I'm rocking now. The pub's closing up. Must be about one. The fat guy behind the bar is just stood there. He turned off the fruit machine before, like that was a sign to get out. Lee comes back from the bog.

'Let's go,' she says.

'Right you are.' I get up off the stool and pull my coat on and we go out the main door that leads onto the main road. Outside slaps my face and I start walking to the chicken place, on auto-pilot.

'Mike. Mike. Come here.' Lee is stood on the side of the road next to a car and she's leaning down and talking into the passenger window then turning and looking at me walking over and then turning back and talking again. She stands up when I get there.

'We can get a lift.' She nods at the car. I don't know who is driving.

'Where?'

'Home. I just need to nip in the club again though. On the way.'

'It's not on the way.'

'I won't be long.'

'Right.' I get in and look at the driver. It's the big guy off the door who twatted me. I don't say anything and neither does he and neither does Lee even though she knows about it. The car does a U-turn and we head into town in silence. He doesn't have the radio on.

The big guy pulls the car up on the no-parking bit of pavement next to the side wall of the club. He gets out and disappears through the door. Lee pulls the seat forward for me and I get out of the back and we go under the blue sign and up the stairs. The girl on the front desk smiles at Lee but not me and we go straight past the TV room and it is full of blokes. The TV is on mute and I can't hear anyone talking. We get to the end of the corridor and go through the door that leads to Ian's office. A girl in heels and a pair of shorts and a bra goes past us and out the way we've just come from. We stop outside the office door and Lee knocks then goes in slowly. Ian is on his phone and he has a bottle of wine on the desk and a glass half drunk next to it. He hangs up when he sees Lee.

'You all right, sweet? Good to see you again.' He stands up and hugs Lee over the desk. 'Did Alex get in touch?'

'Yeah, Ian. She text me before.' Lee sits down. I stand in the corner. Ian's got a picture on the wall and I stare at it and listen to them.

'Good. So you know then.'

'Yeah.'

'What's been said?'

The frame round the picture is cracked and there's no glass in it.

'Nothing. But it's inside. It's still there.'

The picture is faded. It's a family stood together in a yard. Three people smiling and with arms round each other. I don't know the faces.

'Do you want a job?'

I want to go closer. The faces make me want to look harder.

'Do you want a job? Michael?' Ian is looking at me. So is Lee.

'What? Don't you want my CV?' I nearly laugh.

'A job. Here. Nothing heavy. Just a few nights that Ray needs off. On the door. Can you open a door, Michael?'

'Just about.'

'It's sorted then. Lee says you're skint and I'll even give you cash so you can keep signing on. You're not in a position to say no.' He stands up and holds his hand out. 'For your kindness, and for my sweet.' He nods at Lee.

'When?' I don't take his hand.

'Sunday night. It'll be quiet. Get here for nine.'

I look at Lee and she smiles.

'Right.' I shake his hand and it feels cold.

'Great.' He sits down. 'Off you go then.'

I go over to the door. Lee stays sat down.

'You coming?' I say.

'No,' she says,'see you later, yeah?'

'Yeah,' I say.

On my way out, the girl Alex comes out of one of the rooms and we have to walk past each other. She makes sure she gets my eye and she smiles, loads of teeth. I look round at her bare back when we've passed and I know I wouldn't really mind seeing that old guy on the floor again, but only if I saw her on top of me again first.

I stand outside for a bit and look at the three standing trees while a few taxis go past and a few pissheads wander around me. I check my phone. I feel like going back to Mand's and getting on the couch again. I look at the door to the club and see a fat Asian guy come out doing up his coat and he does a little half-run when he turns up the road and walks away from where I'm stood. He checks over his shoulder a few times then crosses the road and a black cab turns up and he flags it down and gets in and it turns left and he's gone. There's no one on the street now except me. I think about that old guy. Whether he was choking or if it was just the cut that did him. Bet he didn't know where he was. He probably got more confused seeing me just stood there before his head hit the floor. I can see the moon. Lee's not coming out and after a bit I walk off.

10

The morning is bright as fuck. The curtains are open and my eyes hurt. I don't feel rough though.

'Dig. I don't feel rough.' I say slowly because my mouth's still tired.

'You didn't have enough then. Or you had too much. Either way I don't give a shit, Mike.' His voice comes from behind me, from his bed in the corner. 'Where's that bird?'

'Lee?'

'No, one of those many other birds you've been charming recently.'

'Fuck off.' I get up. 'I don't know where she is.' I go downstairs for a piss then I make a brew for me but not for Dig.

I get out of the flat and walk across the car park to the shop. The bins behind the takeaways stink even in the cold. There's a girl sat on some steps outside the door of one of the other flats and she's watching me walk while she smokes even though she looks too young. She's got pyjamas on, and her pasty white legs are poking out of the bottom of the pants and into some dirty white trainers that are too big. An old black man is walking towards the shop in slow motion. He's staring at the ground and some cars coming in through the entrance have to brake and wait for him to get to the pavement. No one beeps but the woman driving the first car says something to the man next to her and moves her hand at the old guy. I get to the shop door at the same time as him and I stop and let him go in first. He doesn't look up, he just keeps his eyes on his feet. He stinks worse than the bins and the back of his coat is covered in dog hair. I go to the fridges at the back and pick up some meat, a packet of grey steak, and I put it inside my jacket. Then I get some milk and some bread and go to the till. I keep my jacket open, I just keep the meat pressed into my side with my elbow, under my coat, and I pay for the bread and the milk and then walk back to the flat.

Dig and me play on the N64 for a bit then he goes out and I make some toast and come back up to the front room and put the TV on and sit down. I eat the toast and watch some shit for a bit then I get up and walk over to the window and look down at the road. There's a woman waiting at the bus stop opposite and a queue outside the butty shop underneath the flat. The pub over the way looks quiet. I want to speak to Lee about my dreams but I can't because she's not here and I'm not ringing her. I woke up in the night again. I saw that old guy from the club on the floor but this time I didn't just watch him. I bent down and I put my hand in the cut in his neck and I could feel his heart beating across my fingers and it felt good. I wasn't bothered about the red pumping out all over my jeans because it felt warm. Then I took my hand out and I let him rest his head on my knees and I stayed on the floor with him. I lifted my hand up, the one covered in him, and started licking it and when I looked down he was gone and I was kneeling there licking my red hand and that girl Alex was where he had been and she had her mouth round me. It all felt so good. I didn't want to wake up and when I did I cried like I had a hole in me.

I go downstairs and go into the kitchen and I open the fridge door and I get the steak out and I put it on the side and I look at it. There's a bit of cloth at the bottom of the packet that's soaked up all the blood that was in the meat. I peel the plastic off the top and slide the steak onto the side and pull out the red square of cloth. It's all cold. The meat is grey and the cloth is cold. It doesn't smell like I want it to. It doesn't smell like I'm with that girl again, in that room that smelt like her perfume and her insides, and the old guy on the floor just lying there stinking hot and deep while he watches us rocking together on the trolley. The meat is cold and it doesn't do anything to me. I hear my phone ringing upstairs and when I answer it it's Mand.

'Michael. Come round, will you?'

'All right. See you in a bit.'

My breath steams out in front of me and the sun makes my face warm while I walk down the hill. Over the walls on each side of the road Sale Cemetery stretches back further than I can see. Trees and stones and some people stood in twos or by themselves looking down with their hands joined together in front of them. I can see some guys cutting the grass by the side of the graves. They've got a yellow van and the back of it is full of tools and tree branches. I want to work down there. With those guys. I want to make the graveyard look nice for the people who come and stand and look down. That would be a job that made you feel good about yourself. You could go home and say I did this today, I made part of the graveyard clean and tidy for the people who come in sad and there's loads more to do tomorrow, the place is so massive the job would never finish and you'd just work around keeping everything right. I would love to work down there and feel like that. It would be quiet.

I knock on Mand's door and she comes to it quickly and opens it and then walks away again so I just see her back going into the kitchen when I step through.

'What are you doing, Michael? Anything?' I can hear the tap running.

'No, just come round. You phoned me, yeah?' I take my coat off. The heating is on high. I walk into the kitchen.

'Yeah. Just thought you might be doing nothing. I need to go to the shops if you want to come. You can stick some stuff in the trolley, if you need.' Mand is at the sink and she is washing her hands. She doesn't look round. I can see steam rising up round her shoulders and it's landing on the window in front of her as well.

'Yeah. OK. Let's go then. I'm not doing anything,' I say and I sit down at the table. Mand turns off the tap and picks up a tea towel that's next to her on the side and she dries her hands.

'Right. Yeah. We'll go then.' She turns the tap back on.

'Shall we walk for a change?' She puts her hands back into the sink and starts rubbing them together. 'Or do you want to get the bus? I'm not bothered.'

'It's nice out there. We can walk, yeah?'

'Yeah. Yeah. OK.' She reaches over and grabs the washing-up liquid off the window ledge and squeezes some of it onto her hands then rubs them together. 'OK. We'll walk it then. Did you go out last night?'

'I was just at the pub with Lee.'

'Again? Do you like her?' Mand turns the tap off and gets the towel and dries her hands.

'Like what?' I say, like I don't know what she means.

Mand puts the towel down. 'You know. She's young, Michael.' She turns the tap on. 'I think she likes you, so be careful.' She starts rubbing her hands under the water.

'Right. Cheers. Are we going then? What do you need?' I stand up and go over to the sink. Mand squeezes the washing-up liquid onto her hands and rubs them together.

'Don't know really. Just bits. I'll make us tea later if you want. Do you want to watch a film or something? Or are you going out?' She rinses her hands off and turns the tap off with her elbow like a doctor. 'You're probably going out, aren't you? But you can have some tea and go out from here if you want.' She picks up the towel and starts drying her hands on it. 'Or let's just go to the shops and then I'll let you go then. You can just walk me up there and then get off if you want. Or you just jump on a bus when we're walking up, get back to the flat, then I can just go do the shopping myself.'

'Mand,' I say when she takes a breath, 'can I have tea

here? I'll stay as well if that's all right. Dig is having some people over and I can't be arsed with it. If that's all right with you.'

She puts the towel down. 'Yeah, OK. That's fine, Michael. That's fine.' She looks at the backs of her hands then turns them over slowly to look at the other side. 'That's OK,' she says to me, 'let's go.'

Mand has bad days like this. She doesn't always ring but sometimes my phone goes and she sounds normal but I can tell that I should get round there quickly. I keep talking to her for another twenty minutes at the sink while she slows down the washing and drying until she puts the towel down on the side and then walks upstairs to get her coat, like nothing just happened. I go over to the boiler and turn the heating off then walk back to the sink and click the lid of the washing-up liquid down and put it back on the window ledge next to a toy giraffe and a green mug from Dublin. There's some washing hung out in the yard and Mand's pot she brought over from the old house is in the corner with some flowers in it. The sun hits that bit of the yard just right and I can imagine it being somewhere else, foreign, except for the red bricks in the wall. The dog next door starts barking as if it knows I'm stood there. Mand says she's going to ring someone about it. Just walking up and down all day dodging its own shit on the floor and barking at nothing. The top of someone's head bounces past, someone cutting through the ginnel at the back to get to the main road or the pub faster, and the dog goes apeshit. I hear Mand coming back down the stairs behind me.

'That fucking thing,' she says, 'I'm going to ring somebody, you know.'

When we're walking to the shop I think about when Mand started going weird. It wasn't that long ago. She rang me in the middle of the night and said could I go round and I said no. Dig and me had only just sorted the flat out and I couldn't keep going back to hers because it was like saying that I couldn't handle stuff on my own. Making my own way and all that. She rang again a bit later and said, please, she needed something doing, she had to go to work in the morning and she wouldn't be able to go and they'd fuck her off if she didn't get something done tonight. Then she started crying and I couldn't really understand what she was saying any more so I jibbed a taxi just round the corner then ran round the back of hers and jumped the wall into the yard. The light in the kitchen was on and I tried the door and it opened and Mand was sat at the table cutting her hair. It was a fucking mess and I ended up having to take the scissors off her and she was screaming at me that she hadn't finished and she was chucking handfuls of hair at me and on the floor and hitting herself in the head with the other hand. I picked her up and carried her through to the front room and put her on the couch and we both just lay there for ages until she stopped shouting and kicking and just drifted off to sleep and I did too eventually and she ended up going to work in a hat in the morning. Her hair's still short now. She reckons it won't grow any longer. I don't think she's bothered. Mand links her arm through mine while we're walking and there is a lot of traffic on the road because it's a match day.

Mand is looking in one of the freezers in the supermarket. She's still got her gloves on from outside so she looks like she works there.

'I've got a job tomorrow,' I say.

'Where?' She doesn't sound shocked.

'At that place. Lee's uncle's place. On the door.'

Now she looks round. 'What is it?'

'A club. A massage place.'

'Fuckssake, Michael. You can't just do something normal, can you? Honestly, touch one of those birds in there and I'll cut it off.' She goes back to the freezer. 'Fucking riddled.'

'It's money, isn't it? If it's no good I'll just sack it off. Easy, yeah? What job do you want me to do, Mand?'

'Do you want pizza later?' she says.

'Yeah,' I say. A girl who looks about fourteen comes down the aisle pushing a pram and the kid inside is bawling. I leave Mand with the trolley and walk off. I go and look at the beer and there's an old guy looking at the wine that looks like the guy from the club and when I see him I get sweaty until I realise it's someone else.

11

When it gets dark outside Mand always leaves the lights off in the front room and just has the telly on. We watch a film in the dark. It's about a guy who gets killed, and his Mrs gets killed, but then he comes back to kill the guys who killed him and his Mrs, and he can track them down through the eyes of this bird flying about, and everyone in it is a fucking psycho except for this one little girl. Mand is asleep before it finishes and I can hear her snoring from the other couch. I get up and turn the TV off and take all the plates and cans off the floor into the kitchen, trying to be quiet. Mand has a picture of us on the wall by the stairs. I look like a right twat. We're pissed up somewhere and I've got my arm round Mand while she's got her arm stretched out taking the photo of us. We're both smiling though, at something I can't remember. When we go out together we don't spend any time talking to each other, just go about our nights but moving between bars and clubs at the same time, waiting for the other one, always getting the same taxi back and then mostly running unless we're too pissed up. I dump the plates in the sink and line the cans up next to the kettle on the worktop. I want a smoke so I go in the shit drawer and pull out Mand's cig tin and her pack of Cutter's

Choice then sit down at the table. I start rolling and I read one of her letters that's lying open. It says that she's being charged £45 plus a fiver for being overdrawn. I go out into the yard and smoke slowly. The dog next door doesn't bark.

When I go back in my phone is ringing. It's on silent so it's just vibrating on the table in the front room. Mand doesn't move when I go in and pick it up. I answer it but I miss whoever it was. The number is withheld. The phone has gone off three times one after the other while I've been outside. I've still got hold of it when a text comes through from a mobile I don't know. There's no message again, just another picture. It's someone lying on their side on a floor in the corner of a room. It's dark but I can see the carpet is blue and the guy on his side has got his back to the camera and it looks like me. Then the phone rings again and it's withheld again. I answer it quickly.

'Who's this?'

'Alex,' a girl says.

'What's with the pictures, what's with the tie and ringing me four times? What the fuck?' I walk through the kitchen and outside while I talk so I don't disturb Mand.

'This is the first time I've tried to ring you, Mikey. The first and last if you don't stop shouting.' She sounds annoyed.

'What? Look, sorry. Have you been sending shit to my phone, pictures?'

'I could if you wanted me to.' That doesn't sound annoyed. 'Really, I just wondered if you were coming in tomorrow? Lee says you are. Says Ian asked you.'

'Yeah, probably. Got nothing better on,' I say. 'Seriously though, since that guy came in I feel like –'

She cuts me off. 'Look, Mikey. I don't know what you want me to say. I need to get back to work, yeah. Just come in tomorrow. You'll feel better.'

'Right, but –'

'Right. See you then.' She hangs up.

I turn my phone off and put it in my coat pocket, hung on the back of one of the chairs in the kitchen. Then I go upstairs and fall asleep in Mand's bed.

In the morning I look in the mirror in the bathroom and my eyes are bloodshot. Mand comes in.

'What you doing today? I've just got some cleaning and house stuff to do.' She needs me to go now. Like she needed me to come round yesterday. She's always like that.

'Yeah, I need to get off myself. I'll just get a brew. Do you want one?' I'm dressed so I start going downstairs.

'Yeah. Cheers, Michael. Cheers.'

'OK,' I say. It looks nice outside. The yard is dry and the sun is on its way round to the pot in the corner. I make a drink for me and her and I drink mine while I listen to some shite on the radio then I shout up that I'm going and the brew is on the side but Mand can't hear me over the Hoover so I just go and make sure I pull the door to after me. I walk up to the main road. There are only a few cars about and nobody else walking but there are two people jogging on the other side, a fat man and a thin woman. A cat comes out from behind the pub and starts rolling on its back on the floor in a bit of sun. I think about going to see Dad because it's close and I haven't been for ages but I need to get home and get sorted for later. I start walking along the main road towards the met stop. It's not the one closest to Mand's but it's one less on the way to town and one less stop for inspectors to get on. Can't be doing with a fine today. On the tram there are two women wearing those black robes that cover them up totally and I watch them and wonder if they're ghosts.

At the flat Dig is asleep in bed and there are some random people asleep on the floor and the TV is on a channel that doesn't show anything on a Sunday morning so it's just a black screen. The meat that I left out in the kitchen is still there but someone has cut it up with scissors and made a meat face on the side with a big smile and they've even done eyebrows with the fat off the meat. It makes me laugh when I see it. The meat face is happy even if it's just rotting on the side. I make a brew and have it black because there's no milk. Out of the window I can see that guy stood by his silver minivan taxi and he's smoking. He reminds me of the big guy on the door at the club but they don't look the same and they both remind me of the guy in the takeaway but they all look different and it's fucking my head up so I look at a green couch in the corner of the car park instead, round the back of one of the shops. Someone's dumped it there and sometimes kids sit on it and smoke weed but mostly it just gets wet in the rain and gets a bit less green each time. When I look back at the taxi bloke he's looking up at the window, looking at me and his cig is just burning in his hand because he's not smoking it any more, he's just staring up. I move away from the window and finish my brew then I go for a shower.

My Nan rings. She says it's nice outside and that I should be out walking. Come round in the week. I tell her yes, Nan. I say I'll come round in the week. She says she hasn't been feeling too clever today. She says that she's glad it's stopped raining and it means that she'll stop worrying about the cat going out now. I say that the cat can look after itself and she laughs like breaking glass then starts coughing and says the cat is an idiot, always has been. I say I've got to go, Nan. She says yes I suppose you do and she says bye and see you soon and then she hangs up. I go and sit upstairs. Everyone's gone now but Dig is still in bed. I stick the news on on the telly. Someone is rioting over something and the police are charging them down and spraying them with water. A man lies on the floor with his legs all scraped and people stand over him waving their hands in the air. It's not over here. It's somewhere foreign. I turn the TV off and move over to the computer.

Dig has left it on like always and I get on the internet and check the football scores from yesterday. Then I do a search for a woman who was on the TV the other day and most of what comes back is pictures of her on holiday with her tits out. I do a search for 7th Heaven. Fuck all to do with the club comes up so I put Manchester at the end. It's listed in something called the Little Black Book and there's a picture of the entrance. I click through a few pages. Dig wakes up.

'Get the fuck off my computer, yeah? I don't want collaring for your she-male porn.'

'Whatever, mate.' I click the window shut and get up and so does he. He stands on the bed bollock-naked and stretches. I sit down on the couch.

'Put something on. Please, Jesus.'

'It's the human form, Michael. In all its glory.' He bends over and shows me his hairy arsehole. 'Take a good look.'

I switch the TV back on.

Later I tell Dig I'm going out and when he asks where I just say out and he gets arsey and thinks I'm going to see Lee because I want to get a grip of her. I go downstairs and out the front door and I hear him shouting down after me that I can fuck off but I know he'll get bored being angry because he gets bored of everything. I jib through the bushes that separate the car park from a side road that runs by the met track and then walk round to the station entrance and down onto the platform. The electronic clock says 20:22 and that there's 8 mins til the next tram. I wait. There's a girl on the other side. She's got headphones on and because it's Sunday night and it's quiet I think I can hear what she's listening to. I listen harder and I can't make it out and then a tram arrives on her side and she gets on and I'm on the platform on my own. I wish I had something to listen to. The sign says 6 mins now in yellow lights. I think that girl Alex will be working tonight and I don't know how I'll feel when I watch some old guy or some fat guy go in the room with her and I know what they're doing in there but I'm stood outside on the door and it doesn't matter what I think anyway because she's just a brass and I just half-fucked her once then watched a guy bleed his self out all over the floor while I stood there with a half-hard dick wishing he'd fallen through the door half a minute later. She is loads older than Lee, probably older than me. The sign says 1 min. I stand up and look down the track for the tram lights and I can see them on the way. When it pulls up I get on near the front and sit down and pull my hood up over my head and wonder why the fuck I can't wait to get to the club.

12

'Good. You're in black,' Ian says when I go into the office. 'And early.' He looks at me. 'Nervous?'

'No,' I say.

'Sure?' He walks out from behind the desk. 'It's easy on a Sunday, Michael. Quiet night. We only have four girls on. Mostly Asian punts. All very ashamed of themselves.' He laughs then. 'Can you do a full shift?'

'When's that til?'

'Half 4. We'll get you some food in.'

'Yeah. No worries.'

'Good. Come on then.' He opens the office door. 'I'll get you set up at the front.'

We walk back through the corridors to the front desk and the heavy door. There's no one in the TV room. The girl on the desk is reading a book and she doesn't look up when we come over.

'Katy. This is little Michael. He's on the door for Ray tonight,' Ian says to the girl.

'Right, boss. No probs.' She still doesn't look up.

'Be nice,' he says – to her, I think – and he walks off. I stand there for a minute. I try to read what the girl is reading but it's upside down. She looks up and catches me.

'Right. I'll talk you through it.' The girl puts her book down and gets up. She's got a pink T-shirt on. 'Here's the monitor for the stairs.' She points to a small TV on the desk. It's got the view from the camera outside, in black and white. 'We let the punts stand there for at least a minute, get a good look at them.'

'OK,' I say.

'Then you open the door and I book them in.' She's got a pen in her hand and she points to the door handle, then to a notepad on the desk, then to a black cash tin next to the notepad.

'Easy,' I say.

'If I'm not at the desk, check the book, tell them which girls are on, book them in. Forty-five for half an hour, ninety for the hour. One-fifty for two girls, and that's half an hour.' She sits down and opens the notebook. 'Alex, Emma, Jessica, Nichelle tonight. The girls decide themselves what the punts can and can't do. I don't move from this chair unless I need a brew or a piss and seeing as you just started you can stick the kettle on.' She leans back and points to a door behind the desk. 'The kitchen's through there. And there's a toilet in the next room.'

'Right. Cheers.' I go to the kitchen and the girl goes back to reading.

The first guy comes up about half eleven. I watch him standing on the other side of the heavy door looking up at the camera like he knows I'm watching him. He's young and he looks like a student. He has his hands in his pockets.

'Not the usual Sunday-nighter,' the girl, Katy, says. 'Remember we have to let him sweat for a bit.'

'Why do you do that?' I say.

'Because right now he's on the edge. He's so excited about getting hold of one of the girls in here but at the same time he's shitting it in case we get raided while he's here or someone recognises him on the way out or we that we just fleece him. Take his money and fuck him off. Got to let him decide if it's worth the risk. You'd be surprised how many get here then run off back to their wives after they've knocked.'

'Right,' I say. The guy doesn't look old enough to have a wife.

'What we don't want is for him to change his mind once he's handed his money over. We don't give it back. No refunds. Some inexperienced punts kick off,' she says then she nods at me. 'Then you earn your money, instead of just making my tea.' She smiles.

I stand up. 'Shall I let him in?'

'Go on then. Looks like he's perv enough for us.'

'Half an hour, please,' the lad says. He's shivering and I don't know if it's the drink or because he's only got a hoodie on and it's got cold out.

'That'll be forty-five pounds, my darling.' The girl, Katy gives him a big fake smile. The guy digs into his pocket and hands over a few notes. 'Have you been to the club before?' she says.

'No,' says the guy.

'Well, my lovely, if you'd just like to go through to the TV room.' She points over to it. 'You can leave your jacket with Michael, if you like. He'll hang it up.'

The guy takes his hoodie off and gives it to me. It smells of aftershave.

'Just go on through and I'll send the girls in to have a little chat with you. Would you like a drink?'

The guy turns in the doorway to the TV room. 'Can I get some water, please?'

'Of course you can, my darling. Michael'll bring it through for you.'

He looks like he doesn't know what's going on but he turns back round and goes sits in front of the telly.

'Just stick that on the door in the toilet, Mike.' Katy nods at the hoodie. 'And get him a bottle out of the fridge. Then she picks up the phone. She's about to dial but then she looks up at me. 'Go on then. The guy's paid his money.'

I walk into the TV room and over to where the guy is sat. I hold out the bottle of water.

'Cheers, mate,' he says. I don't say anything. His face is grey and his eyes don't look at mine. He looks at the bottle and then at the TV then back at the bottle. He takes the top off and has a swig.

'Cheers, mate,' he says again.

'It's OK,' I say and I go back to the front desk.

Katy keeps reading. The young guy's left but there's two others in the TV room now, a fat Indian and a skinny white guy in a suit. The Indian guy's got an earpiece for a mobile phone in. I watch the monitor on the desk for anyone coming up. I hear the girls go into the TV room and start chatting to the two guys. I can hear one of the guys laughing and I look round and see the skinny guy get up with one of the girls and they go off down the corridor. The fat guy is still sat down talking and there's a girl on each side of him on the couch. They've got their hands on his legs and they're smiling and looking at him straight in the face and when they talk they lean in and whisper to him and he laughs. I look back at the monitor and at the bottom of the stairs someone pops their head round the door frame and looks up. Then they go again and no one comes up. Katy is still reading. I look back at the TV room. Alex is standing in the room in front of the fat guy and the two girls on either side of him. The fat guy nods his head and stands up and says something and goes off down the corridor with Alex. The two other girls come out to the front desk and go through to the kitchen. I hear the kettle start to boil.

Lee knocks on the door. I can see the top of her head on the camera. She's got her hood pulled up but I know it's her because of the coat she's wearing. I don't wait, I let her in.

'Mike. Hiya. How's it going?' She's smiling and she smells like drink. 'I knew you'd come in, I told Ian.' She puts her hand out and squeezes my arm. 'You OK?' she says.

'Good. Yeah. You all right?'

'Yeah. Been at the Piccadilly. Not bought a drink all night.' She smiles again. 'Loads of pissheads in there.'

We just stand and look at each other for a minute then Lee sees Katy. 'All right there, Katy-my-matey, you all right?' Lee is louder than normal. Katy looks up and smiles.

'All good, little Lee. You all right?'

'Sound, yeah, sound.' She turns back to me and Katy carries on reading. The skinny guy in the suit comes out from the corridor and asks for his coat. I get it from the back of the toilet door for him and he leaves. Lee looks after him and watches him go down the stairs on the monitor and she looks like she's smelt something rotten.

'Right. I've got to see Ian. Is he in?' Lee says.

'He was before. Do you want me to come through with you?'

Katy looks up. 'She can find her own way, Mikey. You stay on the door.'

'See you in a bit then,' Lee says and she gives me these two little slaps on the face. 'See you later, Mikey.' She walks off.

A few more guys come in, then there's no one for an hour. Katy orders a Chinese in and the guy who delivers it is young and he's looking around the place with big eyes and he looks at me probably thinking I've got the best job in the world. I keep a straight face so he can't tell. The food is good. I didn't know I was hungry until it turned up. We eat at the desk and we don't really talk. I see guys leave, looking down at the floor. Most of them stop at the bottom of the stairs and then pull their collars up or their hoods or just look outside quickly before they step into the street. It gets to three o'clock. Katy books a taxi for three of the girls and they all come out together and go down the stairs saying 'Goodnight, new guy' to me and laughing. Lee and Alex come out to the desk. Lee is quiet now. Alex is in normal clothes and she's got her hair tied up and she's carrying a big bag.

'We're getting off early,' Alex says. 'Dead tonight. All the pervs are skint.' She laughs.

Katy starts counting the money in the cash tin and writing something down in the notepad. 'Here.' She gives me some money. 'For the full night.'

'Cheers,' I say. I count it quickly. Seventy quid. 'Cheers,' I say again.

'Well deserved. Not a sniff of trouble.' Ian comes in from behind us all. 'Nice bit of work, Michael. Fancy some more?'

'Defo.'

'Tomorrow then. Same time.'

'Nice one.'

'Got the tin, Katy?' Ian says.

'Here,' she says and she passes it to him.

'Michael. Do us a favour, mate. Grab this.' He gives me the tin. 'And these.' He gives me some keys. 'Lock the tin in my office, would you?'

'Yeah yeah.' I start walking.

'We'll be here. Don't be long,' he says. I think that Lee says something as well but I don't catch it.

All the lights in the side rooms are off and the lights in the corridor are low and everything is pretty quiet. I can hear the notes in the tin sliding about and I wonder how much is in there. I get to the office and go in. I don't turn the light on, I just drop the tin on the desk and then come out and it takes me four goes to get the right key for the door but I lock it and put my shoulder against it to test that I've locked it properly. I turn to start walking back up the corridor and I'm a couple of steps on and there's a noise behind me. Like someone's knocking on one of the doors, only softly though. I turn round and walk back past the office door to the end of the corridor. It turns right there and there are no more doors off it until the very end and that looks like a fire exit. I walk up to it. Someone's left it open and I can feel the air from outside coming in through the crack. I push it open and see the night outside. There's a metal platform and a staircase that leads down into a yard at the bottom and that's walled off all around. It's just a dirt yard, no flags or anything. I go out onto the platform and I can hear the knocking noise again. It sounds like it's coming from down in the yard so I let the door rest to behind me without shutting it and I walk down the staircase and I try to be quiet about it.

13

When me and Mand used to play when we were kids I always wanted to be one of those guys from films who can do all those martial arts, high-kicking the fuck out of everyone and making loads of mad noises. Mand hated it because she had dolls to play with but I always wanted to drag her outside and practice setting up fight scenes with loads of rolling around on the ground and fake deaths and we'd always use this brush that Mam kept in the yard as like a staff or something. I'd get her to hold it then I'd go like I was charging at her and grab the handle and she'd have to roll backwards and I'd jump and go flying over her head like she'd thrown me that way in the fight. It was the best move and I think Mam shit herself once when I made her come outside and watch and we did that one. There's all sorts of broken shit in this yard like a pile of bricks in one corner and not one of them is a whole one. You'd cut yourself up good on this ground as well, if you wanted to do some fight scenes, because there's broken glass everywhere and when I get to the bottom of the metal staircase and step onto the ground I crush some glass under my trainer and it scratches against the stones. The walls round the yard are high enough that you can only really see the sides of the buildings around and the night sky. There aren't any windows overlooking it either.

There's a bit of wind out here and the knocking sound comes again. Underneath the metal platform, on the side of the club, ground level, there's another door and it's not closed. The air is swinging it backwards and forwards and every now and again it catches the door frame and knocks like it wants to come in. The paint on the door is the same blue as round the front but it's all peeling off and there's a panel of glass in it that I can't see through because it's blacked out. I can't see anything inside. The wind gets up again and I can smell something. I put my hand on the faded door and push it and step into the room. Something catches and drags over my shoulder and I grab and pull it and a light bulb comes on in the middle of the room. Everything goes white. The walls are clean and white and it makes me feel cold just standing in there. Even though it's cold outside, it feels like the room is doing it. I pull my hood up and I let the faded door go so I'm properly inside. The bulb doesn't have a shade on it and it's really bright. The room is long and there's one door off it that is closed tight in the back corner. There are metal racks of empty shelves along both sides of the room. On the right of the door were I'm stood is a chest freezer like the one in the flat. The floor is tiled white. It smells of bleach and something. Right in front of me is a drain set into the tiles. I think I can hear something like running water coming up from it. Underneath the light bulb there is a metal table, some sort of metal, clean and shiny on four legs that have wheels. I walk over to it and touch the top with my hand. It's freezing. I bend down and run my hand down one of the legs. It's as smooth as anything on the way down but when I come back up my finger catches on something raised that's round the side I can't see. I lean under the table and look where my fingers are. There's a brown line a few inches long and it's raised from the metal of the leg and it's got a round bit at the end, a droplet, like someone's dropped paint on it, like the paint's slid down the leg and then dried like that. I rub my finger over it and some of it flakes off onto the floor, rusty. Probably is rust. It might get damp in here, if the door's not shut properly. I stand up. I go back to the door. It's rust on the table. Not paint. Or something. It feels like rust. The bleach smells like metal underneath. My eyes hurt like it's too bright in here. I pull the light cord off and I get out and pull the door shut tight behind me and it holds.

'Michael. There you are, mate.' Ian is on the platform above the yard. 'Where've you been?'

I take my hand off the door handle. 'Nowhere, boss. I thought I heard something out here. The fire door wasn't shut properly.' I make my voice sound like I'm not bothered but I'm sweating like fuck. 'Nothing out here though.' I start to come up the stairs. Ian starts coming down to me.

'Nothing out here? Good. Nice one for checking though, mate.' He gets to me on the stairs and puts his arm round my shoulders. 'Dedication. That's what I'm talking about.' He takes me back up to the platform at the top and we stop. He makes me face him. 'You all right, Mikey-boy? You look a bit peaky.'

'Think I'm just tired, Ian. Long shift. Late night, yeah?' I say.

'Right, right. No problem.' He looks at me like he's going to say something else.

'No problem,' he says again. We're stood there for a minute and then he lifts his head up a bit and breathes in deep and squints his eyes like he's smelling something dead nice.

'Let's go.'

We don't say anything on the way back to the front desk. Lee and Alex are still stood there. Katy isn't. Lee has her hands in her coat pockets and she's got her head down. Alex looks at Ian when we come back in and then she starts smiling.

'At last,' she says in a voice like she's laughing. 'Can we all get off now?'

I look at Lee. Her face looks sad. We go down the front stairs first, then Alex, then Ian and he locks the front door and locks the shutter down when we're at the bottom. There's a silver taxi outside.

'See you kids tomorrow then,' Ian says. 'Same time, Michael.' And he walks off towards the arena.

Alex gives Lee a hug. 'See you soon, little girl. See you soon.' She squeezes her again. Lee keeps her hands in her coat.

'And see you tomorrow, mister doorman,' she says to me and she winks. Then she pulls the minivan door open and gets in. I can't see the driver. She gives us a big fake wave when it starts off but I don't even think Lee sees it because she stays looking at the ground.

'You coming to mine?' I say to her.

'Please,' she says. She sounds far away.

I start walking for the bus station and Lee follows and I hear the silver taxi accelerating away from the lights behind us.

I'm shaking. The bus isn't due for twenty minutes but I don't think I could walk back now anyway. I sit in the bus shelter and shake. Lee is stood a little bit away staring up at the sky. She looks bigger and smaller than before, both at the same time. She looks like a statue. I hold my arms round my belly and try to keep my legs still. Lee makes me wish I could be still. I'm jealous of her standing there and staring up. I want to be still and staring like the night around us doesn't matter and nothing matters. The old guy bleeding out onto my bare feet doesn't matter. Or the guys who come to the club and the girls they take into the rooms. Like they don't matter. Just staring at the sky. The metal and bleach and the way that Ian looked at me on the fire escape. Like that doesn't matter. It doesn't matter that I'm back there tomorrow. Lee is next to me. I didn't hear her move.

'Are you cold?' She says it in a slow voice and she's looking through me.

'No.' I hug myself tighter and put one foot on top of the other and press down to stop them both moving about. 'Just feeling a bit off. Probably that Chinese I had.'

'I feel on,' she says, 'not off. Everything is on. It's so

bright out here.' She turns around and walks off underneath a street light, stops and looks up at it and she's still again.

She leaves behind the smell of something. I'm jealous of her. My guts ache.

14

I'm up early and my back is fucking killing because I slept in the chair again and let Lee have the couch. Dig was out all night but I didn't want to use his bed. Lee is still asleep and I stick my jeans on and go downstairs. Out the kitchen window I see the silver taxi parked outside but there's no guy stood there smoking. I don't know who picked Alex up last night. I didn't see who was driving. I try to think of the guy's face but I can't see him right, just the smoke from his cig and his little eyes that look black in my head. My phone goes off and it's Mand wanting to know how last night went. I text back, Good ring you later, but I know I'll leave it and let her ring me. I make two brews and go back up. I don't put the TV on or the computer, I just wait for Lee to wake up herself.

I don't feel rough any more. I didn't sleep good though so I'm tired. Lee came in and lay down and she's not moved since. Proper out for the count. I kept looking at her in the dark and trying to nick some of her sleep for myself. When I closed my eyes I saw that room. Whiter than white and all the steel shining bright. Sometimes. I'd roll over and close my eyes again and it'd be different. Not white. Not bright. Brown and red everywhere. Dripping and drying and hanging off the edge of the table and chunks of meat on the shelves and the fridge wide open but I didn't dare to look inside it. Then something started crawling at me along the floor and I saw it was the old guy with his throat open and he was reaching for me. I sat straight up then and shouted, only I wasn't back in the chair in the shitty flat I was back in the white room and I was sitting on the table and Lee was stood next to me smiling and looking through me. Fucked up. I kept saying that, fucked up. Then I opened my eyes and the flat was back and Lee was asleep and the sun was nicking in through the curtains but I couldn't decide if here was better or if I wanted to be back in that room to see what happened.

'So we're going where?' she says. She is loud again and happy.

'My Dad's,' I say. I don't know why I'm going. I haven't been round for ages and Mand never goes. 'Just want to stick my head in.'

'Cool. I'll be on my best.' Lee is skipping along next to me, not walking normally because I'm rushing and she's just keeping up. 'You going to work tonight?'

'You were there when I said yeah to Ian.'

'I know,' Lee says. 'So it's all right then?'

'It's fine. Yeah. Are you coming in again?'

'I doubt it. Don't really need to.'

I stop. 'Lee?'

She carries on a bit then spins round on her heel. 'Yes?' she says it in a posh put-on voice.

'I don't know what happened. When I was there. Before Ian wanted me to work.' It comes out like I'm a retard.

She comes over to me fast and puts her hand on my chest. 'Don't say anything, Michael. Don't talk about it,' she says it low. 'Don't start talking to me about it.'

'OK,' I say, 'OK.'

'None of it matters, Michael. Put your arms round me.'

'OK,' I say, 'OK.'

'That's it. That's it,' she says. 'None of it matters.'

The road is busy with traffic but I can't hear it. I can just hear my heart beating loud in my ears and Lee whispering.

'It'll be different, Mikey. It can be different.'

The dogs are out in the front yard when we get to my Dad's but they don't bother with us because they're fighting over some food. When I ring the bell it's like he's been waiting for us by the door, it opens that quick.

'Michael, you little bastard. Get in here,' he says and he coughs all over us. 'Too long lad, too long. Get in.' He waves us past. I go first into the dark hall and left into the front room. The TV is on loud. I sit down on the couch and Lee sits next to me. Dad shuffles in and sits in his chair.

'And what brings you to see you old man, eh? Money, isn't it?' He leans forward and points his finger when he says money.

'I don't need money, Dad,' I say.

'Well, I haven't fucking got any so I can't help you anyway.' He sits back and throws his hands up and lets them smack down on the arms of the chair. Some dust rises up.

'I don't need any money, Dad. I've got a job.'

'Some sort of shit you're in, then? Need your old fella to back you up?' He starts looking around the floor by his feet.

'No, Dad. Things are OK.'

'You can tell me, son. Don't matter what shit you've pulled. Ah!' He grabs a bottle up off the floor and unscrews the top then starts looking around again, for a glass.

'I'm not into anything, Dad. Just come to see you.'

He doesn't say anything. He's trying to find a glass. I see one on the window ledge. I get it and pass it to him. It has something dried in the bottom of it.

'Nice one, lad,' he says and he fills the glass and knocks it back then fills it again. 'Drink?' he says to me.

'No. Cheers.'

'Drink, tart?' he says to Lee.

'No, thanks,' Lee says. She looks down.

Dad stares at her for a bit and has another swig from the dirty glass. 'What job you on, then?' he says to me.

'On the doors. At a club.'

He nearly spits. 'You? Is it a fucking kiddies' club?' He laughs and then coughs. 'They better hope there's no trouble while you're on.' He laughs again and he drops the glass out of his hand and it spills on the carpet. 'Fuckssake.'

I go to get up and to go over to get it for him off the floor.

'Sit the fuck down. I can get it myself,' he says. Lee moves a bit where she's sat. He gets the bottle and has a drink from it and leaves the glass on the floor.

'So you've just come to see your old man, have you? Even though I've not heard off you for months. Or that slag sister

'You're quiet tonight, Mikey-boy. I mean quieter.' Alex laughs again when she says it.

'Just eating,' I say and I hold up the bit of pizza in my hand like it's proof.

'Fair dos,' she says.

Someone knocks on the door.

'I better get back,' Alex says, 'speak to you later, yeah?' She winks at me and goes. I finish the pizza I've got in my hand and put the kettle on again before I open the door.

It gets to half two but the time goes slower than slow. I get up and go for a piss. I don't need it. I'm bored. The wall behind the toilet is cracked white and I can see the plaster underneath. The flush sounds loud in the small space. In the kitchen one of the girls is sat at the table with a cig. She's on her mobile. The noise of her tapping on the screen fades up as the toilet flush dies away. The strip light on the ceiling flickers. I hear two voices out at the desk so I go through. Katy is on her own.

'Lee's just come in,' she says but she doesn't look up. 'She said hiya.'

'Right,' I say and I sit back down and put my hands in my pockets. 'She said she wasn't coming in tonight.'

'She's in every night, Mike.'

'Right.'

In the TV room, Alex laughs her fake laugh and gets up, holding hands with a guy who is shorter than her. I hear her heels go off down the corridor and then a door shuts.

'Has she come to see Ian?' I say to no one.

'Who?' Katy says.

'Lee.'

'What else?' she says.

At four we're empty and Katy puts her book away and starts counting the cash tin and writing stuff in the notepad. I go into the kitchen and empty the bin and turn the light off. Alex and the two girls who were on tonight are sat in the TV room in their normal gear, talking. I come back in carrying the bin bag.

'Just stick that by the door and go see what those two are doing. I want to get off,' Katy says.

'Lee and Ian?' I say.

'Yes,' she says.

I go past the TV room and the girls in there start whispering, then I hear Alex laugh and they whisper again. I check the rooms on my way down to the office and I turn off some lights that have been left on. One of the rooms smells sweet and hot and I see a red dot in the corner when I flick off the light so I go in and it's the wall heater so I turn that off as well. I get to the office eventually and there's no one in there. I go round the corner and the fire escape is open. Out on the platform I can see some orange from a street light lying in the yard and it lights up a broken bottle propped up against half a brick. Something starts moving around underneath the platform.

'Michael. Michael, Michael. My man. Here again?' It's Ian. He steps out from under the stairs and into the orange light. His eyes are wide. 'Here again?' he says and he holds his arms out. 'Why?'

'Katy asked me. She said she wants to get off,' I say. My voice is small.

'Did she now? We'll be going soon.' He puts his foot on the first metal step. 'There's something I need you to see first.'

'What?' Softly I hear my heart in my head.

'Come down here,' he says.

I don't move straight away. I feel hollow.

'Come down here, Michael,' he says it again and it floats up to me in the dark.

I take the first few steps down. 'What's up, boss?' I don't know if I say it out loud or just in my head. He doesn't say anything but he stands back when I get to the bottom and lets me step down into the yard.

'This way, lad.'

He goes over to the door under the stairs. The pale blue peeling door with the white room behind it. I can see the light is on inside because the black shade on the door's glass panel is grey.

'You need this, Mikey-boy. Come on.'

He opens the door and the light and white inside is blinding in the dark outside. He stands black in the doorway for a second then steps through and I follow him in and out of the night.

It smells beautiful inside. I can't see anything past the light. I put my hands on my face and I think my eyes are melting out of my head but then I know that I'm crying. Not making any sound though. Just like something is leaking out of me. I wipe the back of my arm across the wet patches and try to see. Lee is here. She is lying on the tiled floor with her back to me and she's holding something in her hands that I can't see. The shelves around the room are still bare and the door at the back is still closed. There is a body on the table in the middle of the room. It is naked. I am awake.

'What the fuck! Ian, what the fuck?' I step back and reach behind me to try and find the door. Then I feel two hands, one on each shoulder.

'Wait. Michael, wait.'

'Wait for what?'

I spin round and push him away. He falls and lands in the doorway.

'You going to fucking kill me, or something?'

He starts to laugh. I hear the metal stairs creak from outside.

'Michael, why would I do that?'

'Because –' I don't look at the table again, I just point at it. I just point at the old guy stretched out on it. 'Because you're a fucking nutter? What the fuck, Ian?'

'It's fine. It's fine, Michael. It doesn't matter.' He gets up slowly and stretches his arms out like he's showing that he hasn't got a gun or anything. 'Nothing matters.'

Something moves behind me and I turn round. Lee is sat up and she's facing me and Ian, angry and weird looking, hair all over the shop, like she's just been woken up. She reaches up to her face and her hand is red. She brushes her hair back and looks up, straight at me, and she smiles. Her mouth is a mess of red.

16

'No.'

I want to get out of the room and get up the metal stairs and run to the heavy door and throw it open and start running like fuck screaming my head off into the middle of the road. Ian doesn't move from the doorway. He's up and he's got his hands pressed either side in the frame, like I'm going nowhere. Lee stands up and she drops something on the floor as she moves. It lands hard and wet on the tiles. It looks like meat. She comes towards me.

'Shhhhhh,' she says.

I sit down on the cold tiles and wrap my arms round my legs and pull my knees up tight to my chest.

Lee stands over me and she reaches down and strokes my head with her red hand. 'Shhhhhh.'

'Everything's different now, lad.' Ian says it slowly, rolling it in his mouth.

People are moving about outside. Ian moves over and Katy and Alex and the two other girls that were on tonight come in. They all look at me with big eyes and straight faces. Lee keeps stroking me. Ian closes the door and we're all inside.

+

Alex goes to the door at the back of the white room and unlocks it. It's a cupboard and she starts pulling out bedding and blankets and throwing them all around on the floor. When they're falling around me onto the tiles I can smell them like they've just been washed but there's something underneath that, the same as underneath the bleach that keeps the room so white. Alex spreads them everywhere so the only cold bit of floor left is where I'm sat, and underneath the table. One of the other girls goes to the cupboard and pulls out a lamp and plugs it in and turns it on in the corner, then goes to the faded door and pulls two bolts across to lock it shut. Ian turns the overhead light off and then him and the girls all sit and lie around me, on the blankets on the tiled floor, and Lee sits next to me and puts her head on my shoulder and the body on the table just stays where it is. They start talking to each other quietly and looking at me sideways. I can't make anything out of what they're saying. It just sounds like someone humming.

'Everything is different. I said it, didn't I, Mikey?' Lee's voice is right in my ear. 'I said nothing mattered, didn't I?'

I nod. My mouth is open.

'I knew when I saw you. When I spoke to you. I knew you could smell it. I knew it was inside you,' she says.

I close my eyes.

'It's in us all. All of us here. And there's others.'

My head's pounding, but when she speaks it does seem easier to breathe.

'We just get on. We have to live. Ian took us all in when

he knew we were like him. We look out for each other. Nothing else matters.'

I puke all over myself, in between my legs and onto the tiles underneath me. They all get up together, quickly. Ian stands me up and the girls move the bedding from round where I was sat and he takes me over into a corner and lies me down. I can hear them cleaning and moving about and they're not laughing or taking the piss, they're just cleaning up my sick like it's nothing. I see Ian walking back over to them as I black out.

It's like snakes. A pile of bodies, lying on and round each other, legs curled round arms and hair everywhere. Ian and Lee and the girls all stretched out over each other, close together near the body on the table. They move slowly, just to bring their hands up to their mouths and hold the pieces of meat against their lips. They drink down the red, and tear off small pieces and swallow. There's no sound, it's dead quiet and they don't speak and I don't even hear them breathing. The smell is there and I know what it is now. The smell of red. Lee carries it on her like a perfume and I like her being around. I like the smell of her and it. I get onto my knees. Lee lifts her head and one of her red hands waves at me. She wants me to come over to where they are. I'm scared. There's nothing else to do.

My phone rings and wakes me up. It's Mand.

'Hello?'

'Michael? You all right?

'Yeah. Yeah.' The room is dark. Someone's arm is on my

chest. My face feels tight when I speak. My mouth is dry. I'm warm. 'Fine, Mand.'

'I'm at yours. Dig said you've not been back from the club.'

'No, I stayed out. At Lee's.' It sounds like a question.

'Didn't know she had somewhere.'

'Well, yeah. She has.' I'm smiling.

'Right. It's dole day, you know.'

'I know. What time is it?' I say.

'Nearly nine.' She breathes out. 'Right, I'm going to work.'

'OK, Mand. Sorry you worried.'

'What?'

'Sorry you worried,' I say again.

'Are you pissed?'

'No, Mand.' I laugh at what she thinks.

'Speak to you later, yeah? Get to the dole.'

'Right,' I say and she hangs up.

No one speaks. We just tidy up. I follow what they do. The blankets go in bin bags and Katy takes them and goes off up the metal stairs. The stuff on the table goes in the chest freezer. The two girls and Lee go upstairs and come back with buckets of water and bottles of bleach and start cleaning everything down.

'You want to go get a drink somewhere, lad?' Ian says.

I look at Lee and she smiles and nods her head.

'You better clean yourself up first,' she says and she points to her mouth.

I go upstairs with Ian and he waits at the front desk

while I go to the kitchen and wash my face in the sink. The water that turns down the plughole has lines of brown running through it. I can smell the night in the heat of the water. My hands feel soft on my face. I dry myself on a tea towel and go back out to the desk to Ian. Lee is stood with him. She comes over and hugs me tight then she walks off.

'Right, lad. Let's go.' Ian goes downstairs and I follow him onto the street and into the grey morning.

'You understand what we did? What we do?' Ian says. We sit in a corner of the pub with two breakfasts and two pints. The place is pretty empty.

I shake my head and drink my beer.

'You know how good it feels?' he says.

I nod my head.

'You feel different? You feel like you're in a dream?' He sits forward. 'You've woken up from one, Michael. You've lifted yourself out of a fucking horrible nightmare.'

'That was real?' I say it under my breath.

'It's so real, lad, that you'll never stop. You're yourself now. Lee knew it and she told us and we showed you.'

'Why?' I don't want to know.

'It makes us live, Michael. It takes away all the shit in your head, everything you worry about. It makes us strong and it makes us weak.' He knocks the table with his fist. 'Things, Michael, things, don't matter. It's what you've been looking for.'

'I wasn't looking. You lot brought me in.'

'Shite. No life. No one. You floated along in a stream of

shit, Michael. We pulled you out because you were drowning.'

I have a drink. This is a film.

'We're the same. And the girls. And others. In this city. Everywhere. No one sees us. We look out for each other.' He drinks. 'You've got a family, Michael.'

'Mand,' I say.

'Your sister?' Ian says. 'Is she in the nightmare, Michael? Is she drowning? The older we get the harder it is to cope.'

'I want to wake her up.' It doesn't sound like my voice. 'I don't want her to drown, Ian.'

'Let's meet her then, Michael.' He picks up his fork and stabs the egg on his plate. The yellow runs out and mixes with the beans. 'We save people,' he says.

'You kill people.' My hand shakes a bit and I trap it under my leg, under the table.

'Course we do. But it doesn't matter. One of them saves five of us, ten of us. They're nobodies. We make sure.' He cuts into a piece of bacon and puts some in his mouth. 'It's a network. We're in the saunas. We're in the bars. We're in the taxis, Michael. We feed them, we give them booze, we drive them around, we fuck them. Then we take something back. And it's good. Isn't it good?'

I'm looking at the floor. 'Yeah.' It's not my voice.

'Yes. Yes, yes, yes, Michael, it's so fucking good. It's the only reason. Nothing else matters for us. See where Mand is? You'd be there, we'd all be there. Fucked, mate. Unravelling. We save each other.'

'Can you save everyone? Do you miss people?'

Ian stops eating. 'All the time, lad. They lose themselves. Pills. Drink. A bottle of each that they chug down through the tears not knowing why the hollow inside them just won't go. When they're doing everything right and it all feels wrong no matter what. They hate themselves. And they're everywhere as well.' He breathes in deep. 'We can only do so much.'

I feel tired all of a sudden and I put my head down on the table. Ian rubs it with his hand then I hear his knife and fork start up scratching again across his plate and I hear him chewing and I remember chewing and drinking in the white room and my stomach rolls and I hold the padding of the seat and watch my knuckles go white.

'You're awake, Michael. You're awake.'

17

Ian gives me his mobile number, tells me to come in later, and leaves me at the pub. A waitress comes over and takes his plate away but she leaves mine because it's still full. I can see drops of grease on the food. I get up and go to the bog. I sit in there for must be nearly half an hour and shit my life out, sweating and cramping and banging my hand on the wall while it happens. Some bloke having a piss shouts, Are you all right? a few times and I shout back something that makes him give up. My arse is raw when I finish. I puke up once on the floor as well. I get out of the cubicle and grab onto one of the sinks for a minute to stop myself swaying. I need to get back to Mand's. A guy from behind the bar comes in and asks me to leave and I tell him I'm fucking leaving now.

Mand is still at work when I get to hers. I go round the back and sit in the yard. I put my back against the big pot in the corner and close my eyes. My guts have settled and I got a bottle of coke from the shop on the way and I'm drinking it slowly. My teeth feel see-through and sharp in my mouth and I sit there and bite bits of loose skin off the inside of my lip and swig my drink. It's bright again. The sun is taking the edge off the cold, thank fuck. I feel like I'm not there, like I'm made of paper. I try to fall asleep but it feels like I just end up sitting there for hours listening to the dog barking and snorting next door and waiting for the sun to come round to where I'm sat.

Mand comes out of the kitchen door. The noise wakes me up and it's dark and I'm shaking.

'What the fuck are you doing, Michael?' She gets to me quickly and bends down and she grabs my face with both hands.

'Waiting for you, Mand,' I say, through the shakes, 'just waiting for you to get back.'

'Get up,' she says, and she starts pulling on one of my arms to help me. I get up and we get inside. I'm cold but I don't feel like I should. Like I just spent half the day asleep in a yard. I feel pretty good. I feel better. Mand puts the kettle on and stands me by a radiator.

'Seriously, Michael, what the fuck?' She says it staring at the kettle while it's boiling, not facing me.

'What? I waited for you. Simple as. Work got a bit manic last night.' I am talking to her about it.

'What, a fight?' She stirs the tea in two mugs.

'No. Look, do you want to come in with me later?'

She turns round, annoyed. 'Why would I want to do that? For a job? You pimping me out?'

'No,' and I say it again, louder, 'no. Not for a job. Just come see what I do, or something. I don't know.'

She walks off into the front room with her brew. Mine stays sat steaming on the side.

+

We watch shit on the TV for a bit. Mand doesn't ask me about the dole but she's sat there thinking about something. I can nearly hear her head going. She makes us some food and I wolf mine. She eats hers slowly and leaves most of it then goes for a shower. I get my phone out of my coat and scroll through the address book to Ian's number and I stare at it for a minute. Then I put my phone away. It's still a few hours til I start at the club. I've got energy. I lie down on the couch and flick around til I find the news. There's a riot. I don't know what it's about. I don't know where it is. They're just showing a bit of film from a helicopter on a loop of people all pushing against a line of police. It's from high up so I can't see them spitting and shouting and throwing things and I can't see the police battering fuck out of anyone. I put the telly on standby and go out the back for a smoke. Last night, in the middle of everything, on the floor, curled around bit of warm meat cut off an old guy's leg, sucking the red out of it like a hungry baby, I looked over at Lee. She was smiling at me. She looked well happy and I saw a bit of a tear catch the light off the lamp in the corner when it slid off her face.

'Mand. I'm getting off now,' I shout up the stairs.

'Right,' she shouts back, 'don't be in my yard tomorrow or I'll call the fucking police.'

It's stayed dry outside but it feels like it might piss down on me any time. I walk fast to the tram stop and get straight on one by luck. Then I'm in town, like that, and I realise I've got the same gear on from last night. Probably stink as well because I've been sweating and shitting and sleeping most of the day. I try to feel bothered but I don't. Can't see that I'm going to get fucked off now. Looks like a job for life. I laugh out loud and some old dear turns round in her seat and eyeballs me. I give her a wink and she tuts and puts her back to me again. I look around myself and there's plenty of people crammed on here and a few of them are giving me the old sideways look. Bollocks to the lot of them. I'm feeling like fucking magic.

I know I'm well early so I jump off at the Gardens and nip into the Piccadilly for one. It's dead. Don't even think there's one other person in there except for me and the girl behind the bar. She was on the other night. Bad attitude. I go over.

'Pint of lager please, my darling,' I say, like one of those wankers you hear in the pub sometimes.

She looks at me like I fed her a shit butty. Mouth open. 'You what?'

'A pint. Any time you like.'

'Of?'

I stir it a bit more. 'Whatever you fancy pouring, princess.' She looks like the Princess of Glassing Me in the Face.

'Oh piss off, mate.' She sticks the pint glass she had ready in her hand back on the shelf above her and walks off down the bar.

'Oi. A drink, yeah?' I get the lump of cash Ian paid me out of my pocket and wave it in the air. 'Dying of thirst here.'

'Yeah, well you should've thought of that before you come in pissing about. Knob.'

Flipped. I leather my hands onto the top of the bar. 'Get me a fucking drink, you ugly bitch,' I'm shouting, 'get me a fucking drink now.'

A door behind the bar opens and some guy in chef's pants comes out and stares at me. I can feel the blood pumping in my head and it's mine and the red from the white room, mixed.

'Get me a fucking drink!' Over and over.

The chef guy picks up the phone on the wall to dial someone. The girl goes back to reading her magazine. Some hairy guy that I didn't see when I came in, sat in one of the booths, shouts at me to keep the fucking noise down. I'm not even angry. I stop shouting and everything goes back to quiet. I feel like laughing again.

'Get out, eh, mate. We don't need another nutter,' the chef guy says.

I walk out backwards, giving them all the eye like some mad arse then when I feel myself hit a door I spin round and pull it open quick and fucking run off faster than I thought I could run, pissing myself like I'm some proper comedian.

I'm still running when I get to the club and I jump upstairs and bang on the door. Ray opens it, then he stands blocking the doorway while he looks at his watch. I'm on my toes looking round him, seeing who's on, who's in. He moves and I step in all casual like I don't care if I'm there or not but really I'm buzzing. Katy is on the desk. Ray sits down on the door chair.

'You're early,' he says, 'you better go through. Speak to Ian.'

I know there's no better about it so I hang my coat up and give the punts in the telly room a wave on my way past to the office. The door is shut so I open it and walk in. Ian is on the phone. He tells them he'll ring back and he stands up.

'What are you doing, lad?' Serious.

'Ready to work, boss. Just here, ready,' I say. I nearly feel like I need to fucking salute him.

'Calm the fuck down, Michael. Calm it.' He walks around his desk to me. 'Enough of,' he waves his hand in the air, 'this.'

'I'm on, boss. I'm set, yeah?' I might be dancing about a bit.

He grabs my shoulders and he makes it hurt. 'Look, knock it on the head, son. I'll give you a fucking slap in a minute.'

I don't know what to come back with. I just look at him.

'You can't act like this.' He's staring me down. 'I know you feel it, but you've got to sort it out. Keep yourself on a level. At least when we're open, when you're out and about.'

'Yeah, but I'm on, boss. I feel good.'

'You will.' He lets go of me and sits on the edge of the desk. 'I'm just saying reign it in though. We don't advertise. That's what I'm saying, Michael.'

I just nod my head and look at the floor. It's what me and Mand did with Mam when she started going off on one.

'We all feel it, lad. You keep it in. You enjoy it, but it's for no one but yourself,' he says. He puts his hands in his pockets. Hiding over, so I look up. Ian is old. The way his eyes look grey and serious, they look older than his face. He moves back round the desk and picks his phone up.

'Get on that door then, lad. Have a good night,' he says and he starts dialling some number.

It's a blur. The night goes so quick. I talk to everyone, toned down of course, but I'm a chatting machine. Katy even puts her book down for a bit and talks to me. Maybe to keep me in line or something but I'm not arsed. We get some food in and the punts come and go, and they all look tired but it's like I've just got up even when it's stupid o'clock in the morning and we're saying see you to the last fella going down the stairs. Lee's in and after I lock up the front I meet her on the fire escape and she hugs me tight. She says she's dead happy and I say I am too, not even thinking about how gay it sounds, and she holds onto my hand when we walk down the metal stairs. Ian and Katy and the girls from the night are there waiting for us in the white room and everything's set up like it was except the thing on the table is a different shape. When it's done I fall asleep curled round Lee with my hand on her belly like I'm looking after something.

18

I'm off and it's Friday, and I want us all to go out. Me and Lee and Mand and Dig and I ring them all and get them up for it. I say I'll get my money out as well because it feels like I'm raking it in at the club. Dig says I'm a fucking flash bastard but he still says he's coming. Me and Dig get sorted at the flat and we get a few beers down us early and meet Lee in the Piccadilly about half seven. Mand turns up about eight and we all start proper drinking then, pints and shots and whatever anyone comes out with. No matter how fucking horrible it is to drink, we give it a go. Lee's ruined when we come out and I'm not far behind to be honest. Think Mand might have even said something to Dig, just a word, something to break the ice for the night, because he's not being too much of a dick. The Gardens are packed with birds and lads dressed up for nights out, walking in every direction like they've all got different places to go to. Sounds like football songs and high heels everywhere. We walk all the way down Market Street to Deansgate and get in the Moon and it's fucking jumping in there. Lee and Mand go off for a piss and me and Dig go to the back bar and get some drinks in.

+

'Battered, mate,' Dig says in my ear when we're stood looking down on the dance floor. Mand and Lee are in the middle of it with some guys round them. 'I'm fucking battered.' He puts his head on my shoulder. I'm watching Lee dance, then Mand. They're both smiling wide and Lee is trying to be all sexy but she's pretty pissed and she's out of sync with the music, which is shit but I don't care. Mand is moving round with her eyes closed, singing every word of whatever it is and putting her hands in the air stretching for the ceiling. I shake Dig off and sit him down on the table behind us.

'Cheers, Mikey. Get us a pint in, yeah?' he says.

I say, 'Yeah, Dig,' and I go to the bar. Some bird stands next to me when I'm waiting and smiles and says hello and do I want to get her a drink. She's a bit old so I say how about you buy me one and she calls me a dick and walks off. When I get back to the table, Dig is gone and he's on the dance floor with the girls shaking his arse round and clapping his hands, fucking loving it. He gets Lee's hands and spins her round and and she's laughing and then he does it to Mand and she's laughing and I'm stood up watching them and smiling to myself just drinking my beer.

A few songs on and there's a bit of a circle come around them now, a bit of space for Dig to make a bigger cock of himself in and he's going like fuck to the music with a bit of sweat on his bald head standing out. Everyone's laughing with what he's doing. Mand and Lee stop dancing properly and they're just swaying a bit watching him go mad. Dig spins round on one foot and nearly falls over then he sees this girl stood round watching him. I could've picked her out for him. He has a grab for her hand and tries to pull her into the circle with him. She doesn't want to go. He moves over to her and starts talking in her ear and she's shaking her head and laughing. I put my pint down. Lee and Mand come up off the dance floor to where I'm stood. Lee nudges against me like she wants me to do something. Dig gets his arm round the girl and he's holding her close in to him while he's talking. She's stopped laughing but she's still shaking her head. Some normal-looking guy comes over and says something to Dig but Dig doesn't look round and the guy just puts his hands out like he tried and then walks off. The girl tries to move away from Dig but he keeps his arm round her. She is looking round for someone. A group of lads come over and I can tell they all know each other because they're all looking sideways at each other and saying things and nodding at Dig. Lee nudges me again and I start walking down to the dance floor to where they are.

'Dig, you cunt, come on. Let's go,' I say in his ear. He's still trying to talk to the girl.

'Get the fuck off me,' she is saying, over and over.

'Come on,' he's saying.

'Dig,' I'm shouting over the music. 'Let's go, yeah?'

'Come on, darling,' he says.

'Get the fuck off me,' she says.

'Now, knob head,' I say and I get hold of his arm and start pulling him away. He looks round and sees it's me. The girl sees her chance and pulls away from him but he spins round quick and grabs her arse, up her skirt. The lads stood around start moving in and I start moving him off to the doors, sharpish. Mand and Lee meet us there and we get out onto the street and they start walking down to the taxis but Dig's just a fucking mess and he's falling about everywhere and I'm trying to pick him up when the first lad comes through the back of me and I hit the pavement with my face.

They kick the shit out of Dig, on the floor. He doesn't even get a decent punch in. I hit a few but get banged down more times and one lad gives me a right boot in my guts that keeps me down for a while and I'm coughing and puking on the pavement. Mand and Lee are shouting for them to stop but it doesn't make any difference really. A few of the lads start drifting away so there's just one left and I go over then with my hands up and I say it's cool, it's cool, he's done mate, and the lad steps back and lets me pick Dig up off the floor and Dig's face is fucked. I walk him over to the girls and they've got a taxi for us, holding the door open, and we all get in. The taxi guy looks at Dig in his mirror but he doesn't say anything and Lee says Swan Street and we drive off.

At the club, Lee and Mand take Dig into the kitchen and I go to the office to check that Ian isn't pissed about us turning up. He sorts us out with a lift back to the flat and says he'll see me on Sunday so it's all fine. He doesn't talk much though, just checks Lee's all right and then sorts everything out quickly like he's got better things to do, which he probably has. The girls clean Dig up so there's only some blood left on his top and a bit that's dried on the inside of his ear. I sit next to him in the back on the ride home and I make sure the window's open in case he needs to throw up but he's quiet on the way back and he hardly even moves. We get out of the silver minivan and get some food and take it up and I dump Dig down onto his bed and Lee puts a glass of water on the floor near him. We all eat quietly and none of us says anything really apart from Mand says that when that lad booted me when I was on the floor I was smiling and laughing like I'd lost it. I say I don't remember and it must be the beer. I think I probably was laughing though. I knew it didn't matter. No matter how much them lads and Dig and Mand and every fucker watching thought it was the thing to remember from that night, how they'd tell their mates in the morning, how they'd feel guilty or like a prick or like they wished they hadn't been there or that they'd done something, there was only me and Lee that knew better. Only me and Lee knew that it didn't matter, and that the blood on the pavement was just wasted time.

19

'Nice,' Alex says, when she sees me sat on the door Saturday night. 'Some one fucked you up, yeah?'

'It's not even that bad.' My face hurts when I speak.

'Whatever,' she says, but she's smiling when she walks off. The club is busy. No one's in a shitty mood though, which is good. Easy night is what I need. The punts all sit quiet and watch the telly. I see them checking their phones sometimes. Like they're waiting for a call. I'd laugh if it rang and they picked it up. Some old guy to his Mrs, yeah back soon, just knocking some twenty-two-year-old's back door in. Love you. A punt catches me looking in and he looks at the ground. The phone goes on the front desk. Katy's in the bog. I pick it up.

'Yeah?'

'Michael.' It's Ian, ringing from the office. 'Michael, lad. Come and see me when Katy gets back.'

'Yes, boss.'

When I go in he's stood up, waiting. He holds something out to me.

'I need you to take this over to a friend. It needs to go tonight,' he says. I take the envelope off him. It's one of them yellow ones with the bubble wrap already inside. It's light, though. Like it's empty.

'Where to?' I say.

'Mia's. Off Princess Street. You know round there, yeah?'

'I know it.'

'Good lad. Just pass this in to Dave. He'll be in the booth by the stage. I'll ring them so they'll know you're from me.'

'Right,' I say. 'Dave.'

'No one else,' Ian says, 'no one else. Wait around if you have to.' He goes back round his desk and sits down. 'Trusting you, Michael.'

'No probs, yeah?' I say and I leave him to it.

A punt comes up on the stairs as I'm going down. I feel like telling him that I work there on the way past but I don't say anything. I can hear the rain outside before I hit the street and I pull my hood up and stuff my hands in my pockets then turn left out of the doorway and start going back down Swan Street. One of my legs feels dead and it aches when I step down on it, probably from the kicking last night. The road's full of taxis rolling past, steamy windows on them from the sweaty bastards with takeaways inside. I want some food. The chicken place down near Mia's is good so I'll go there after I've dropped this shit off. I can feel the envelope next to me, inside my coat, but I take one hand and push against it just to check it's there, like it's important. It might be important. Take something from here to there. Easy. Three girls stagger past me holding their coats over their heads and I can see the cheeks of one of their arses her dress is that small.

+

I jib over the road between a few cars and go right onto Oldham Street. The door to the City is shut but I can hear a woman screaming something when I go past and the lights are on behind the curtains. A bus goes past with no one on it except the driver. I cross at the junction and get past Gulliver's and the Castle, and some little bald guy's being sick outside there and taking drags on his cig in between throwing up. At the next junction I cross on a diagonal to get under some scaffolding and out of the rain but it only lasts a few steps and I feel it hitting me again. There's some flats on the other side of the road and two guys are stood on one of the low balconies just looking down. I look up at them while I go past and one of them looks like he's going to say something but he doesn't and I keep on going. I get to the lights at Dale Street and start crossing but when I'm halfway some dick sat waiting starts revving his engine and nudging forward at me. I try to look to see who it is but the headlights are too bright so I just get out of the way and he wheel-spins behind me and gets off up the road and I hear someone shout something but the engine's too loud for me to hear it.

I get into the Gardens and go across the bridge, over the fountains, then walk over the tram lines past the met stop and then through the bus station, and I get onto the corner near the amusements. At the taxi rank up on my left I can hear a scrap going on but I don't want to watch it and I don't turn round, I keep walking. I stay on the right side of the road for as long as I can because it's under cover. Portland Street to the junction with Princess Street and I turn left. Harter Street on the right. The door to the club is at the end. Green. Closed. The road is short and dark. On a red brick building next to the club entrance there is a sign high up that says in red on white, TO LET – HIGH SPEC OFFICES. I step over a few trails of piss on the pavement where people have tucked themselves into the little door-ways and fire exits for a burst. I can't always piss in a urinal but I can always piss in the street. So can these fuckers. I get to the door and I knock and I wait.

It's smoky inside. I forgot what that was like. All the smoke that hid the stink of piss and sweat and sick and bad booze and cheap perfume and desperate lads. It smells like smoke in here and underneath that it smells good. Like 7th Heaven. The bouncer is fine with me coming in when I say where I'm from. He knows I'm not pissed up. He looks at my face a bit longer than normal, at the few bruises, I suppose. There's a woman with glasses, who's probably Chinese, sat behind a desk and she looks at me when I come in.

'Want to leave your coat?' she says.

'No,' I say.

The glass door into the bar looks like it should be in someone's front room, going through to a kitchen or some-thing. The carpet inside is a mad mess of red and green and brown. There are curtains hung around the walls but I don't know what colour they are because the lights around them are red and they make everything dark red. I go over to the little bar in the corner and get a beer and sit down.

Might as well chill for a bit, the rain's going nowhere. It's busy. Some lads are sat round a big table looking through the karaoke book and writing down songs and there's fucking loads of empties on their table like they've been there hours. They're shouting over each other trying to grab the pen and the book, laughing about it. There's a few couples dotted about. One of the couples, the guy is talking to another girl who's stood over by where the two of them are sat. The girl stood up is young-looking but she's got these massive tits and they're out on show, and the guy loves it, but I think his Mrs loves it as well. Near the toilet doors there's another big table and it's got some Chinese guys sat round it and they're not really talking, they're just smoking and they have a girl bringing drinks over to them on a tray.

Some bird gets up to sing. The lads on the table all start cheering and she waves at them and she's got a cheeky little grin on her. The words come up on a pull-down screen and most people in the bar start singing along with her and it's a good job because she's shite and pissed. I finish my beer and go over to the booth by the stage. There's a guy in there. He's got a green cap on and his face is lit up by a laptop screen.

'What is it, mate?' he says, 'What you singing for us?' He looks at me then. 'Fucking hell, you all right?'

'Fine, yeah. It's nowt. Look,' I say, and I start to get the envelope out of my pocket, 'Ian wanted me . . .

He grabs my arm and speaks fast. 'Put that away. We'll go upstairs. He waves over to someone at the bar and then gets down out of the booth. He's pretty small when he stands next to me. 'This way,' he says and he goes up some stairs just behind the booth that I hadn't even noticed before. While we're going up, the girl on the stage finishes her song and everyone goes mad like it was the best fucking thing ever.

It smells sweet upstairs. It's just another big room, with a bigger stage than downstairs at one end and some tables set up in front of it. It's darker, though, and the stage is lit up. It's got a curtain across it as well, like there used to be at the cinema or like there's a play on. I can't hear the music from downstairs, just some weird shit coming out of the speakers around this room, sounds like something from a kung-fu film. Most of the tables are full, pretty much all blokes but there's a few birds dotted about. Some other girls are walking round giving drinks out.

'This way, lad,' Dave says, and I stop staring round and follow him through a door at the side of the stage. There's some people behind the curtain setting something up but we're past it quick and through another door into like a locker room. A few girls and a guy are in there, dressed up like I don't even know, mad make up on, even the fella, but they look at me like I'm in the wrong. One more door and an office, like Ian's. Dave sits down and points to another chair so I sit down too.

'You got the envelope, lad?'

'Yeah.' I pull it out from my coat and put it on the desk.

'Good stuff.' Dave takes it and puts it in one of the desk drawers. 'Thank you.'

'No probs,' I say.

'You're Ian's man, then?'

'Yeah,' I say, 'yeah.'

'All right.' He's looking at me close. Not just looking at the mess on my face. 'Fancy another drink? Show's going to start in a minute.'

The girls on the stage are like something else. Not strippers. They're dressed old, old-fashioned, things in their hair, feathers, loads of colours. The music is cheesy. I'm sitting to one side of the stage with Dave, on my fourth pint, and these girls keep coming on, always a bit different, and they've got little dances that they do and sometimes there's a guy with them who they take the piss out of. It's all meant to be funny, I think, because the people watching laugh and clap sometimes. The girls are fit. One comes out with all these balloons on herself and pops them slowly until she's proper naked but by that time she's covering her tits and her arse with two big fans. She gets a big clap. One guy stands up and whistles.

'What do you reckon?' Dave says. He's not looking at me. He's turned away from the stage. He's looking over my shoulder.

'Fuck knows,' I say.

'Well, it's nearly done now,' he says. Don't know if he's put out. I turn round to try and see were he's looking. At the back of the room, just at the side of the bar, there's a chunky guy sat on a chair by himself. No table. He's got his fat head against the wall, keeping it straight. Pissed up to fuck. A girl from behind the bar comes out and swaps the guy's empty pint glass for a full one.

The curtain's been across for a bit after the balloon girl finished but it starts sliding back now, slowly. Some music starts up that I sort of know but I don't know where from. The back of the stage is painted up black, full moon up in one corner, some stars and that. Like the sky outside, only if there were no street-lights. Everyone starts clapping even though fuck all's happened yet. The music gets a bit louder. Dave moves around on his chair and I can see his head going from the guy at the back of the room to the stage, then back to the guy. Two girls come on and they've got masks on and just some bras and knickers and they're pushing a box on wheels. The masks a blank, plain white, just with holes for the eyes. The box is big enough to fit someone in. Dave leans right into my side.

'It's magic this, mate,' he says, like he's trying to whisper but he can't. 'Fucking magic.' He leans back and he's got some mad grin on his face.

The girls stop the box in the middle of the stage and then walk away from it and stand on either side, dead still, looking out at the tables. The music stops and the front of the box opens and there's another bird stood in there. Her mask is black and it has eye holes and a mouth, turned up in a grin like Dave's. She walks out of the box and stands at the front, in the middle. Then the music gets going again and all three of them together put their hands up to the eye holes, like they're got the sun in their eyes, and they're scanning the room. The crowd in the room's gone quiet, everyone waiting to see what's happening. Dave scratches the side of his face and I hear the sound of it. The girl on the left-hand side stops still, staring at something. Then the girl on the right stops. Then the girl in the middle stops and they're all staring somewhere off the stage, into the crowd, and I look at Dave and I already know where he's looking, and he's looking at the guy sat on his bill at the back, and that's where these three on the stage are looking as well.

The girl in the middle points at the fat guy and a light from somewhere shines on him. He looks like he doesn't notice at first, then one of his hands comes up and rubs his face and the pint glass in his other hand slips and falls on the floor but there is only a little bit left in it and it sinks into the carpet. His face looks sweaty under the light. He sits forward a bit and puts his elbows on his knees. The crowds start clapping. Dave is clapping. The fat guy slips to one side a bit and nearly comes off the chair. Someone laughs. The girl in the black mask claps her hands and the two girls in the white masks step off the stage and start walking through the crowd. The crowd clap a bit harder because they know this guy's got picked. The white masks get to him and lift him up, one under each arm, and they start going back to the stage.

They get him up there and stand him on his own in front of the box. The door on the box is open. The white-mask girls walk off the stage. The girl in the black mask goes over to the fat guy and holds his hand. Then she starts dancing round him, rubbing herself on him. A couple of guys in the crowd start cheering a bit. Dave starts laughing. The fat guy smiles and he's looking a bit embarrassed and he's swaying side to side as the girl's dancing round him, like he's too pissed to stand still, like she's taking his balance away, dancing round him. Then the girl leans in a bit and she must say something to him and his face changes. It goes straight and he's not smiling or embarrassed any more. Looks like he's going under. She keeps dancing, spinning round him, putting her hands all over him and lifting her bare legs up, keeping him on the spot and he's swaying more and he's starting to look around, not just focussing on her. She leans in again and says something and his eyes go a bit wider and he tries to step forward but she gives him a little push back and that's all it takes because he's that fucked. Dave laughs again, harder. The girl disappears round the back of the guy, then her hands slide round the front of his face and cover his eyes and she sets off spinning him round slowly. She's just steering him round and it looks like all he can do is stay on his feet. The guy's not got a fucking clue where he is. Then his mouth starts going and he's saying something, some words that I can't hear, and no one in the crowd can hear him because the music's got real loud all of a sudden. His mouth is just going fast and his hands are balled up by his sides and the girl spins him faster and she's guiding him backwards to the door on the box and they get there and some people in the crowd are stood up and shouting and laughing and the fat guy's just spinning and saying words I can't hear and Dave's next to me and he's clapping and laughing his head off and then the girl jumps up onto the fat guy's back and she's still got her hands on his eyes and he's still spinning and she's got her mouth right by his ear, and they spin together into the box and the fat guy's mouth opens wide and the door shuts.

The music stops and the two girls with the white masks walk back on slowly and they stand either side of the box. One of them opens the door on the front and the box is empty. The crowd goes fucking mad. Dave stands up and he's screaming and shouting and clapping his hands and punching into the air. The girls in the white masks bow and the curtains slide shut and the lights come up. The crowd calms down, and they all start shouting their drinks to the girls stood round the edges of the room.

'Good, eh?' Dave's smiling.

'Eh?' I say. My head feels mashed.

'Beer?' Dave says.

'No, you're all right,' I say. 'Best get back.'

'No worries. Come back though. The show carries on,' he says, and then he's looking round at everyone in the room, 'once these fucks have gone home.'

I get up and walk to the stairs. A barmaid walks past me and she goes over and picks up the chair where the fat guy was sat and she carries it away.

When I get out I go to the take-away over the road. The guy in there asks me how's your night been, matey, and I tell him I'm working and I tell him where I work, when he asks. He stops talking to me then and he just looks at me now and again while he's serving other people. When my food's ready he doesn't charge me.

20

Mand needs me round there. Monday morning. I get the
bus from the club to hers and get through the door and see
she's not downstairs so I go up to her room and she's on
the bed and her eyes are rolling about in her head and she's
thrown up some yellow shit all over herself. She's smashed
her mirror. The frame's still hanging on the wall but there's
glass everywhere. She's got a little piece of it in her hand
and maybe on purpose she's been squeezing it because her
hand is wet and covered. There are empty packets next to
her bed. I pick them all up and stuff them into my coat
pockets then I get her dressed and get a taxi sorted to take
us to Trafford General. The woman on the phone asks if I
can calm down. I ask Mand what she's doing and she says
she's sad and her breath smells of sick.

The waiting room smells of damp and bleach. Not like the
club. It smells rotten in here. There's a little kid and his
Mum sat over from me and he's got a tea towel wrapped
round his hand and he's crying into her side, but he's being
quiet about it at least. The TV on the wall is on mute. I'm
tired. It was quiet at the club. I saw Lee and she said the
shit they do at Mia's has got a name but I'm fucked if I can

remember it now. Dave's got people with him there, just like Ian does at the club. Lee said they're mates. She said the envelope was probably money. She said was I OK and I said yeah and she went then. Funny how I only really see her now when we all go down the back stairs to that room. Funny that I'm bothered. Someone shouts my name out, and when I look up there's a doctor or a nurse, or some guy in a uniform anyway, stood there wanting me to go with him.

Mand's behind some curtains. When I go through there's definitely a nurse in there looking at Mand and writing something down on a bit of paper on a clipboard. She smiles at me, then at the guy behind me and she goes out. Mand's got a tube up her nose and some stripes down her face, make up from her eyes I think. Her mouth's hanging open and she's asleep.

'Your sister will be all right. You brought her in in time,' the guy says. 'An hour later and she might not have been.'

'Right,' I say.

'You can have a few minutes with her then she needs some time. We're going to keep her in for at least a few days,' he says, and he goes out.

Mand has got one of those things stuck in the back of her hand. She looks pretty white. There's nowhere to sit down. There's a bed with her in it, and a curtain. Someone outside shouts fuck off well loud and something sounds like it's got knocked over. Mand's hair is stuck to her head because she's sweaty. My phone goes off in my pocket. I'm really tired. Mand's eyes are still closed. They've got her in a blue sheet thing. I don't know where her clothes are. When she gets them back I don't know if they'll still have sick all over them. She doesn't know I'm stood next to her. She doesn't know where she is. Probably doesn't give a shit. She wouldn't be able to hear me if I said something. I turn round and go back out through the curtain. If I got her to the club it'd stop happening. The guy's outside.

'That was quick,' he says. 'Hard to see her like that, isn't it?'

'Yeah,' I say, but it isn't because I've seen her like that before and Mam was like that too, worse, before she died, and I just walk off.

I get a coffee from a machine in a corridor then go outside. The plastic cup is thin and the coffee is hot and my fingers burn so I put it down on the floor next to me and get my phone out. I ring Lee.

'Hiya, Mikey.' She is excited.

'All right,' I say.

'Are you working later? I'll be in,' she says.

'Yeah. Probably. Mand's not well. She's in hospital.'

'Aw, sweet, is she OK? What's up?'

'Just not well, she'll be in there for a bit.'

'You're still coming in though? Sure Ian wouldn't mind if you were off for a bit.'

'No, I'll come in.'

'All right then, but if she needs you there then Ian would let you go, you know?'

'She's not going to need me here, is she? What will I do? I can't wake her up, can I?'

Lee doesn't say anything for a bit, I can hear the wind down the phone because she's walking.

'Don't worry, yeah. Just don't worry,' she says, eventually.

'Right,' I say and I hang up. I bend down to pick the coffee up off the floor and a tear drop falls off my face and lands wet on the back of my hand, and the coffee cup looks blurry.

I get the bus to the edge of Trafford Park then walk back to the flat from there. I go into the supermarket and get some sausages and a loaf and when I get in I make some butties. Dig is out so I put the TV on and watch a few DVDs that make me laugh. I drink about four brews one after the other. Then I lie down. I wake up later because Dig is shaking me.

'You're fucking crying, mate,' he says. He looks mad. I get up and find my coat and go straight out to the club, even though it's still light outside.

On the tram a woman is shouting at her kid because it won't hold on to some handle and it's going to fall over and she won't be looking after it if it does. I stare at the stones at the side of the track and they're a grey blur with a dot of something pink or green or blue in it every now and again. A paper or a can of some drink. I get off at the Gardens and bob in the supermarket on the side of the Arndale for tea and coffee and sugar and milk for the club because Katy texted me before about it and I remembered somehow. The girl on the till smiles at me nice when I get to her so I read her name badge while she's scanning the stuff. Some smackheads are getting thrown out by the security guard, a woman and a man. The woman's giving it the big show shouting her mouth off but the guy just wants to get out and try robbing somewhere else and he's got his head down. The check-out girl shakes her head and says every day but I don't know if she's talking about the scrotes getting thrown out or that they just come in the shop every day, because they might not always be on the rob. You have to pay for a bag so I just carry the stuff out myself. Those two are stood outside arguing. I push through a bit of a crowd that's around them and go back up Market Street towards the club.

'All the time! All the time!' The woman is screeching it. 'I'm tired, Terry! I'm fucking tired!'

21

I don't start for ages at the club so I get there and set myself up in the kitchen with some papers out of the TV room and just keep making myself coffee. I sometimes say yes to a cig off the girls who come in on their breaks and I brew up for them but we don't say much else to each other. I ring the hospital and they say Amanda's condition has not changed, but they expect her to be awake and communicating sometime tomorrow. Ian comes in and sits down.

'We've got one tonight, lad.' He says it quietly.

'What?'

'We've been watching someone for a while and I want to sort it tonight.' He looks at the front page of the paper on the table. The story is about a missing girl. I read it before. He looks back at me. 'I want you to help me out.'

'Right,' I say.

'The guy's young. But he's no one. Nobody. Nothing to miss. You get me?'

'Yeah,' I say.

'We'll get him in with Alex. He comes in about half ten so it's all about normality, yeah? There'll be other punts in.'

'Yeah,' I say.

'Yeah?' he says. 'You're not exactly filling me with

confidence, Michael boy. Any questions perhaps? Some response that makes me think you give a fuck?'

'No,' I say. I know what we're doing. I don't want to think any more about how we do it.

'You'll just follow my lead, yeah?' Ian grins on that. 'Easy, yeah?' He gets up. He goes over to the door but he doesn't go out, he just pushes it closed and puts his back against it. 'After Alex has fucked him, she'll take him for a cig on the fire escape. He always wants a cig after he's got his end away. Me and you wait in the office. She says she needs a piss and leaves him there. We get a grip of him out there and get him downstairs and then we do him, Michael.' He smiles wide. 'He don't come back upstairs. We all go see him later. That's how it works.'

I hear all that even though my hands are on my ears like I'm propping my head up on the table, pretending like I'm listening hard but I'm trying to not listen at all really.

I sit on the door and I feel sick. Katy is reading so she doesn't talk to me. The door feels heavy when I open it for punts. They're all the same. Their faces are all the same. They're excited and glad I opened the door for them and glad I don't ask them questions and glad when I say you pay here and point them to Katy and she does her act like they're really welcome and not pervs at all, gents or something, she says to them. There's a steady flow. Lee gets in and Katy's not arsed if I go for a quick brew with her so we go to the kitchen and I boil the kettle, again.

'You OK?' Lee says. 'You OK being here?'

'Yeah. Ian wants me to help,' I say.

'Oh,' she says, and she looks at the floor.

'Mand's just the same. I rang up.'

'Good. That's good. I'm hungry, Mike.'

'I know,' I say. 'I am too.' I know I'm too hungry to be at the hospital.

'Do you mind?' Lee puts her hand on my hand and squeezes it a bit.

'No,' I say, 'I don't mind.'

She smiles at me. White teeth and blue eyes and her head looks small. I didn't notice that before. 'Thanks,' she says, 'thanks, Mikey. I know it's not the best thing. Ian doesn't like us helping.'

'His girls,' I say.

'Suppose,' she says.

We sit there for a bit longer then she gets up and goes to the bog. When she comes out she stands behind me for a minute as if she's going to say something else to me but she ends up staying quiet and just going out, down the corridor. Going to see Ian. She doesn't stop for a drink.

When the punt gets to the top of the stairs, Katy calls me over to the screen on the desk and we stare at him through the camera. He keeps his face to the floor but I know I haven't seen him before. The top of his head is showing through his hair and the shoulders on his coat are darker than the rest of him so it must be raining outside. He's rocking, side to side. Katy is staring at me now, not the monitor.

'You getting the door, or what?'

I get it and he steps in quickly. He's small. He scratches

the back of his head a lot when he talks to Katy and he doesn't look at her, just at something behind her that I can't see. His voice is quiet. He hands over some money and then he turns round to me and he's holding his wet coat out. It's brown and it looks like a dead dog. I don't want to take it off him so I pretend I haven't seen and I sit down on my stool and start picking my fingernails.

'I'm sorry, sir,' Katy says, and she must come round the desk and take the coat. 'Please, go through and make yourself comfortable.'

He smiles and says something quietly and I can hear him shuffling off into the TV room.

'Pussy,' Katy says. I know she's talking to me but I keep my head down. When I do look up she's gone.

When I was a kid I got battered in the park. Six lads got hold of me and kept kicking til I was fucking flat out. They were bigger, probably older. One of them was the brother of some girl that had got them down to sort me out. I was playing with her first and we got round the side of some wall, out from where people could see us anyway and I was sweating I was that excited and I tried to stick my hand up her skirt. My guts were all over the shop and my stomach went mad when I was ducked down there with her and even madder when I stuck my hand up there and felt something hot. She didn't move first of all and I just kept my hand there, flat against her, and I could feel that in my hand and the blood in my head pumping like fuck. Then she made this little noise and started crying and ran off and I stayed were I was, hoping she'd come back. My legs went dead after a bit. When the lads got there I couldn't stand up. When they went again it was the same but I was bleeding pretty bad. Mand came out and found me for tea because Mam was feeling bad and she wouldn't get out of bed to find me herself. Probably made her worse seeing me when I got back. Mand took me into her room and the light was weird in there because the sun was beating but the curtains were pulled shut. Mam didn't turn over or anything. We walked round to where she was lay down and she had her eyes open so she saw me and she just started crying but there wasn't any noise. Her eyes just leaked and shook in her head.

'Michael.' Katy is stood next to me. 'Ian wants you.'

I get up and start walking to the office but my legs are heavy. The TV room is still pretty full. Everyone in there is a fucking pervert. I go past one of the girls in the corridor, I can't really remember her name even though I've eaten meat out of her mouth on the floor downstairs and she's told me that I'm beautiful. She smells sweaty. The rooms are looking full, most doors shut and the usual noises coming out. I think I can hear Alex shouting something. The office door is open a bit so I go straight in. Ian is stood up, probably waiting for me.

'You set, lad?'

'Eh?'

'Fuckssake.' He walks round his desk then bangs his hands down. 'No fuck-ups. No fuck-ups, Michael. Lee brought you in and you wont fucking let the girl down, you hear me?'

My head is pounding and I can see Mand with that thing sticking out of her hand but she's still covered in sick.

'You don't let her down. We don't do that. Get yourself sorted out, yeah? Be fucking ready, Michael.'

'The guy's not got a clue,' I say. It sounds like I say it to myself.

'Give your head a wobble, eh, lad. The guy's not got a clue? It's a good job. Know why? Because in about fifteen fucking minutes you and me, Michael, you and me we're going to kill him.' He slaps the desk again. 'And then later on, we're all going to go down there and we're going to fucking eat him.'

'It's fucked.' I'm sweating everywhere.

'You're fucking right it's fucked, lad. But you know what? It's what we are. Fucked. With or without it. Learn to be fucked, lad.'

'I'm sick, Ian. I feel sick.' I sit down on one of his chairs on my side of the desk and put my head in between my legs. He walks back round to me and he puts his hand on my shoulder and keeps it there. It feels warm.

'Just hungry, lad. Just hungry.'

22

Ian and me sit quiet in the office til we hear Alex take the punt past the door. She's talking too loud, letting us know what's going on, spinning the guy some shite about how good and how great and how she loves it when he comes in – dead serious. If they take it in they must be soft. Probably just part of the game though, they both play it, don't they, not just the girls.

'Come on, Michael,' Ian says, 'let's get this shit done.'

'Right,' I say but I stand up slowly. Ian goes to the grey cabinet on the wall and pulls something out of one of the drawers and it's thin and it's made of metal. He gives it to me. I push it in the front pocket on my hoodie and my hand shakes while I do it. He goes to the door and flicks the office light off then pulls the door open a bit so some of the light from the corridor sneaks in over his shoulder. I can smell cigs. I'm standing in the dark with a knife in my pocket. I can hear high heels and Alex walks past and I see her just turn her head to the gap in the door and wink and she's gone. Ian goes out into the light and then I go after him.

It's cold in the corridor and colder again when we get round the corner and I can see the punt out on the fire escape with his back to us. The sky round him's got some stars in it. I'm fucked if I can remember stars from anywhere and I feel like I should stand there for a bit and look at them. I pull my hood up. Ian doesn't try to be quiet or anything now, he just walks up and out of the door onto the metal ledge and sparks up a cig himself, like normal, like what he does every night when he wants a smoke. There isn't enough room for me to stand with them, three along, so I kind of walk through them two and stand down one step on the stairs. I face up to them and look straight at the punt. He doesn't look at me, he's not really registering us, he's trying to look like he's relaxing, like a bloke who just got his end away, cool as, except he paid for it and we all know that, and even if he thinks we've both paid as well then that just makes us all the fucking same anyway. Ian speaks and it makes me jump.

'You all right there, fella?'

The punt blows some smoke out over the railings and I watch it while it disappears. He leans on one elbow and looks at Ian, half looks at him, stood next to him, but then when he talks, he talks to his feet.

'Good, yeah, pal,' he says, and he has a quick look at me then down again. 'And yourself?'

'Not too bad, not too bad. Decent little place this, isn't it?'

Ian turns himself to face the guy properly. He's already nailed his cig and he flicks it off into the yard underneath us and it sparks up off a pile of bricks.

'I like it,' the punt says. 'Don't you work here?'

'I own the fucker,' Ian says, loud. 'Ian.' He puts his hand out. 'Glad you enjoy our services, mate.'

The punt shakes Ian's hand once. 'Well, I best get myself off. Good to meet you, Ian.' He pulls his grey jacket round his belly.

'Don't go now, fella, not yet,' Ian says. I shift my feet round and the whole staircase creaks. 'I know you're a regular right, and, you see, we –'

The sound of the door down the corridor opening, the one that splits the office from the club, smashes out into the dark and the punt jumps and drops the end of his cig. It rolls down his pants and onto the floor and leaves a black smudge on its way. Then, Alex's voice.

'Ian. Ian! Fucking get in here!'

'Shit.' Ian ducks inside the doorway and starts off going then turns and pops his head back out, to me. 'Just look after our friend, Michael, yeah?' He looks at the front of my top, at the pocket. 'Don't fuck about lad.' Then he's gone back inside.

'Look after me?' the punt says, 'I don't need looking after, cheers, I'll just go.' Then he goes for the door.

'Wait. Just wait, yeah?' I say it slowly because I'm thinking and talking. 'It might be a raid.'

'The police?'

'Yeah,' I say. It might be.

'Fucking hell, fucking shitting fuck.' The guy starts ranting and he comes right up to me and puts his hands up like he's surrendering. 'The fucking police, I can't, shit, fucking shit.'

'We can get out down there,' I say and I point into the

yard. It might be the police. It doesn't even matter. I can hear loads of shouting from inside but not what anyone's trying to say. The punt looks to the doorway then at me and down the stairs. He steps towards me.

'Please help me.'

'What?'

'Please. I can't get caught here. I can't.'

'All right, mate. All right. We can go.' I step down one stair. He starts to follow me. I step down some more and he keeps coming. I can hear him sniffing over the shouting. A girl is screaming inside as well. I step down into the yard and go to the door under the stairs. The punt stays behind me.

'Cheers for this, mate, thanks,' he says. 'I can't be here.'

I don't say anything back to him. I turn the handle and open the door and let him go first. I don't put the light on.

'Where now, mate?'

I close the door behind us. I can see him in the dark, looking round, rubbing his hands together. Wiping his nose on his sleeve.

'Where to, mate?'

I put my hand in my pocket and go a bit closer to him.

'Is there a light in here? Mate?'

I get hold of the knife and take it out.

'What the fuck? Put a light on, yeah? Fuck!'

I try and grab him round his neck. He spins round and I lose him and he swings his arm up and his elbow or something leathers me one in the face. I drop the knife and I'm on my knees. He kicks me. We don't say anything. He breathes hard and so do I and I lie on the floor. He finds the door and pulls it open and he's gone. I hear the stairs creak. I get up and go back into the yard. My nose is leaking everywhere and it's all over my hands. I look up at the stars and I can hear someone screaming again, upstairs. It sounds like Lee.

23

Lee is screaming. A guy's got her by her hair and he keeps throwing his hands around while he's shouting, and he's pulling her head backwards and forwards with him. She's got her eyes shut and her hands stuck in her hair trying to take some of the weight off it. The guy's big, built. He's half-dressed. He's got a tattoo on his neck. Everyone's in the TV room except there are no punts left, just Ian and Alex and Katy and some of the other girls on, and there's this guy holding onto Lee with one hand and he's got a knife in the other. He's shouting and raging and doing his fucking nut and Ian is shouting back at him as loud, with his arms out, and Alex is crying and screaming, and Lee is screaming harder than before and her feet are hammering up and down on the floor, trying to get her away from the guy or trying to stop feeling her hair getting ripped out. None of them even looks at me when I go in. The punt from the yard is gone. Must've run straight through. My face hurts.

'Stop struggling, bitch!' The guy drags Lee back to him and bends down and puts his knee in her back and pulls her head towards him. 'Fucking sit there.' He gives her a slap with his other hand. He catches her with the handle of the knife in his hand and she starts bleeding from just underneath her eye.

'Get off her! Get off her!' Alex is dribbling she's crying that much.

'Trying to fuck me over, eh? Trying to fuck with me? I'll kill the fucking lot of you,' he's screaming, high pitched, 'the fucking lot of you! Do you know who the fuck I am?'

Lee is just in her bra and knickers. She's tiny. I start walking over to her and the guy.

'Back the fuck up, lad, I'll snap her fucking neck, then yours.' The guy spits all over me. He's still down behind Lee with one hand in her hair.

'Michael, lad, don't.' Someone behind me.

I take the knife out of my pocket and have it facing down in my fist. The guy's not even seen it. I'm close enough.

'One more step, you prick, one more!' He starts bringing his knife up, slowly, on its way to Lee's neck.

I fling my hand down as hard as I ever have and the knife slips into his shoulder, up to the handle. I can't hear any screaming or shouting or crying now. Everything goes dead quiet.

The guy's breath is hissing. He lets go of Lee and puts both hands up on the knife I've stuck him with, and he's confused. She crawls a bit to me and puts her arms round my legs. I can feel her shaking and how cold she is through my jeans. The guy starts to stand up. He puts his hands against the wall and starts walking round the room, over to the door. He's leaving prints in red along the wallpaper. Alex comes over and drops to the floor around Lee and then

Katy comes over too and then I can hear some crying but it's soft and there are words in between the sniffing. I step back, next to Ian. The guy stops on the wall, over halfway to the door. He's staring down at the floor. He's got his back to us so it looks like he's not got a head. He takes a breath and it sounds like a whistle. Then he starts again and he makes it to the door and then through it and he slaps both his hands on the front desk and has another breath, then he gets over to the heavy door and opens it and he takes the first few steps down and we just watch him go until the top of his head is gone again. Ian sits down on the couch and puts his hands on his face.

'Shit. Shit. Shit.'

I look at the hand prints on the walls and Ian on the couch and Lee and the girls on the floor. Then I look at my hands and they're redder than ever.

I wonder if Mand's woken up yet. I wonder if she's woken up in the dark and if she's happier than she was or if she's just as sad, or more. Ian locks the heavy door and makes us all go into the kitchen. Someone puts the kettle on. Lee goes into the toilet for a while and Alex stands by the door like it hasn't got a lock. Ian is stood with his back to the room, with his hands on the worktop and his head is down. A couple of the girls are sat next to me, round the little table, and one of them, Helen, is crying quietly while Katy strokes her hair and says things like shhh. My hands are drying and getting stiff.

'What the fuck?' I think I say it to myself but Ian turns around.

'Exactly, lad. What the fuck was that?' The girls are looking at me too. I can see them out of the side of my eye.

'What?' I say. The toilet flushes and Lee comes out and her and Alex go and stand by Ian.

'You stabbed a guy,' Ian says.

'You wanted one stabbing.'

'Don't be fucking smart, boy.'

'Ian.' Lee grabs his arm. 'He thought he was doing right. The guy was nuts, yeah?'

'I know, darling, I know. But he did wrong. The guy's gone.' Ian's face is all creased up. 'The guy's gone. We need to move.'

'What? Move where?' Lee comes over to me and she puts her hand on the back of my neck.

'What's gone on downstairs, lad?' Ian says to me.

'Ian?' Lee says.

'Nothing,' I say.

'Nothing?' Ian says to me.

'Ian?' Lee says.

'Nothing,' I say.

'Fuck,' Ian say to no one.

Lee takes her hand off my neck and slaps them down at her sides.

'Ian, for fuckssake! What do you mean move?'

'Just get all your shit together. I need to make some phone calls. Help them out, yeah, Michael?' Ian goes out the door. It bangs shut behind him, ten times too loud in the quiet and I jump.

Someone carries on crying while we all sit there saying nothing.

+

Lee takes me into one of the rooms and closes the door behind us. I stand in the corner by the shower. She goes under the trolley-bed and pulls out a bag. It's like one that a posh girl would use for school, it's big and square and there's one strap to go over your shoulder and the fasteners on it are gold and it's leopard-print coloured. Then she goes round the room picking up shit and putting it in the bag. A pair of shoes and something else that is black material. She puts them away quickly.

'Is that all your stuff?'

'Yeah.' She keeps fussing round the room. She's been round it four times. The little table next to the trolley-bed has got a white bowl on it, full of johnnies. There is a guy's jacket on the floor near me.

'Thank you.' She says it while she's bent down checking under everything.

'It's OK.'

She stands up and puts the bag on her shoulder and zips it up. She comes over to me to say something else but I don't want to listen to anything else, thank you will do, so I go round her and go out of the door. She doesn't come after me straight away.

24

'We're done here.'

Ian is stood at the heavy door. His face looks different. We're all stood or sat listening to him. Someone's taken the appointment book off the front desk. The girls have all got bags. The taxi driver's turned up. He stares at me while Ian talks. He's smoking and because we're all inside it tastes heavy in my mouth. My hands are sweaty.

'You all know people, yeah?' Ian says. 'We've all got somewhere to go?'

No one says anything, no one nods or moves but that means yes, I suppose.

'Right.'

He walks over to the camera monitor on the desk and goes to turn it off. Something moves on the screen before his hand gets to the button. Someone starts coming up the stairs. Then a few blokes are coming up the stairs, one after the other. The first one gets to the top. He's got his hood pulled up. I can't see his face. It looks like he's going to knock on the door then hits the camera with something and it fizzes and goes off. One of the girls gets up from where she's sat.

'We're closed, mate.' Ian puts his head against the door

when he says it, so they can hear. No one says anything back.

'Yo. We're closed, yeah?' He shouts it. Someone starts knocking. Six times. Fast and hard. Then quiet.

'Fuck off,' Alex shouts from behind me, but her voice is shaky.

Someone knocks again. Five times. Harder. One of the girls steps back from the door. Ian bangs his hand against our side of the door a few times.

'Get lost, yeah? Find somewhere else. Just up the road –'

But he doesn't finish telling them where to go. The door rips apart and I feel like I've gone deaf. I see Ian spin round with a look on his face like he's staring at somewhere in the distance. His shirt is gone from round his belly and there's a big red mouth instead. He puts his hands on it, but it's too big to close, and then he falls on his face and he doesn't move. It smells like bonfire night. Someone grabs me and starts pulling me backwards past the door to the TV room. I can hear again and I can hear screaming. It's Lee who's got hold of me and I nearly fall on my arse she's pulling that hard. We go round a corner and I just catch some blokes running in through the gap where the heavy door was and one starts beating the shit out of the taxi driver with a bat. I don't know who they are. They've got masks on. One is a clown. One is a cow. One is a Freddy Krueger and he's got a gun. The sound rips out across the room again and one of the girls pretty much falls in half. I don't see her hit the floor.

I get myself turned round and we're running, me and Lee,

towards the back door, to the fire exit, fast, and we don't say anything, it's like we're just thinking the same thing, to get to that door. Someone shouts behind us.

'Lee! Lee!' It's Alex, she's just behind and Lee looks back quick and slows down a bit to wait for her. I slow down too and watch while Alex catches up then Lee grabs her arm and the three of us batter through the door to the back of the club. We get past the office door and two guys come into the corridor behind us and they're shouting to whoever that there's some here, there's some here, so we all look round shitting ourselves and Alex trips on something and she hits the deck. One of the guys gets to her and jumps on her with both feet. The other one gets there and kicks her in the face. Her bag gets knocked along the floor and all her stuff comes out. Knickers and bras and shoes and make-up spray along the carpet. Lee stops and starts to go back. One of the guys looks up and sees her and starts coming for her while the guy behind is on his knees laying into Alex's face with his fist, shouting and spitting all over her. I pick Lee up round the middle and back through the fire exit door and onto the platform outside. Both guys are walking towards us now, nice and slow like they know we've got nowhere really to go. Alex rolls over on the floor and I think she looks at us but her face is such a fucking mess that it makes me feel like puking over the side and onto the bricks in the yard. The door behind the blokes swings open and another one comes through.

'Time to go, boys, it's getting hot,' he says. 'Fuck these two.' They all turn and go back through the door. I let go of Lee and she slides her back down the railings of the platform til she's sat down and then she puts her head back and screams at the sky and I just stand next to her doing nothing.

I try to get Alex down into the yard before the fire spreads to the back of the club. I roll her onto her back and stick one arm under her legs first then the other under her head and I'm lucky she's light and I stand up and carry her out, past Lee who stays sat on the fire escape. I go down the stairs and Alex's head bobs on each step like the purple stains on her face are agreeing with what I'm doing. I put her down where the ground looks pretty soft, where there's no bricks and I take my hoodie off and roll it up and put it under her head. I look up at Lee. Some black smoke is drifting out of the doorway and over her head.

'Lee. Come down.'

I put my hands in my pockets because it's dark and it's cold.

'Lee. Come down.'

'Fuck off.'

'Come down. The club's going up.'

'I'll watch.'

'Watch from down here.'

I see her head move as she looks up into the doorway, straight ahead.

'Where's Alex?' she says.

'She's down here.'

'Dead?'

'Yeah.' She is. She felt dead when I carried her.

'She shouldn't have died.'

'There's no rules, Lee.'

She stands up. She starts on the stairs and they creak. She keeps her hand on the railings all the way down and stops at the bottom. She looks at Alex, on the floor.

'She's so pretty.'

'I didn't want her to get burned,' I say, like it would matter.

'Thank you.'

She comes over to me and we have this sort of weird hug where she puts her arms round me and I just lean down into her because my hands are still in my pockets. I can smell fire now. We sit down in the corner of the yard and watch until the smoke coming out of the door is too thick and too black then we climb over the wall and get round the front onto the street. The road is empty and quiet and I think I can hear the club cracking and falling down inside. Lee phones 999 while we walk to the bus station. We don't go past anyone and we don't say anything for a long time.

25

Lee stays outside near where the ambulances come in and I go to the reception and they say Mand's been moved to a ward now and they tell me how to get there.

'But you can't see her just now,' the woman says, 'she'll be sleeping. It's not visiting hours. It's not even daylight.'

I say I'll wait and she frowns at me. I sit on one of the chairs in the waiting room. The woman looks up from her computer every now and again to check if I've gone but I haven't. Lee comes in after a bit and sits next to me. She puts her head on my shoulder. We both fall asleep for a bit. Alex's purple and red battered face screams at me. I jump awake and Lee's mouth is wide open. I stare at a magazine on the table next to us. My arm goes dead around Lee's back. I'm thirsty. I'm hungry. I'm tired. The clock doesn't tick but it flashes. The TV says a missing girl has been found. Her parents aren't happy. She was in a river. A man she knew might have done it. She'd have known him after that. A policeman wants help. A photo of the girl comes up and she doesn't look real. It's a model having a photo done of a girl on a night out. She is smiling too wide. She has done nothing wrong. I fall asleep again.

+

Someone tells me I can go and see her. The walk to the ward takes ages. I go past an old lady who's looking out of a window at a bit of brown garden. All the tiles on the floor are the same and all the tiles in the roof are the same, except the ones that are missing and I can see pipes and electric cables when I go underneath them. Nobody else is visiting yet, I'm the first one, the nurse on the desk says. She smiles at me but it's one of those smiles that's like a sorry. She takes me over to Mand. I sit in a chair that's got red pads on the arms, and yellow foam sticking out where one pad is ripped. Next to the bed is a set of drawers. The wood on the side is peeling off a bit. There's a jug of water and a plastic glass on top. The jug and the glass are cloudy. The water is dead still. I can hear a TV coming from somewhere. It's too warm. Lee went outside because she was hot. She went to get us a drink. Mand is awake.

'Michael?' she says.

'Yeah?'

'Remember when Mam took us to Tatton Park? That time?'

'No.'

The windows in the ward are covered over with thin mesh that's been painted over that many times that some of the gaps have been filled in with off-white blobs. The sun is out, outside.

'It was hot. We went in the car. Shit-car. Before she got the new one.'

'Right,' I say.

'We called it shit-car. I hated going out in it. I used to put my head down in the back if we went past someone we knew. She wasn't bothered.' Mand breathes in deep. 'My head is killing.'

'Do you want me to get someone?'

'Remember the park bit there? They had a zip line. It was massive. Wood chips all over the floor.'

I don't know what she's on about. 'Yeah, Mand.'

'There was a lake. There was an ice cream van. There was this big tent set up for some sort of fair.'

The drip in her hand looks sore. The skin in between her fingers is cracked and red.

'We stayed until it closed. Mam had butties and some cartons of drink. Me and you didn't fight or anything.'

I look up at the ceiling. It's cracked and yellow. I can see Mand staring at me, her head is turned on the pillow.

'That was the best day. I was so tired when we got home. I think you were gone as soon as the car started. If I could go back then, I'd die in my sleep that night.'

One of the cracks over us goes from one side of the ward to the other. Mand turns her head away from me and she's looking up at the ceiling too. We both stay like that until a nurse comes over and says it's time for me to go and that Amanda needs some rest. I don't know Mand's crying until I look at her properly because she's doing it with no sound.

'Let's go to that place, Mike. Mia's. See Dave.' Lee is waiting outside for me. 'Tell him what happened.'

The sun is cold, but it's high and bright and different to inside the hospital. Lee grabs hold of my hand and I let her pull me away from the doors and over the road to the bus stop.

'Actually,' she says, 'shall we just walk back into town. It's nice, isn't it?' She starts off. I stay at the bus stop. I've only got a T-shirt on. She stops and turns round.

'Come on. You'll fucking freeze.'

'So, let's get the bus.'

'Come on.' She starts off again. I kick the ground and start following her. When I catch up she gets hold of my hand again.

'What's Mand like?' She says it fast.

'Bad. And she'll be out tomorrow.'

'Are you going to take her home?'

'I don't know.'

'Are you hungry? I'm starving, Mikey.'

'Yeah. I'm hungry.' My guts are still though. Calm. I feel hungry in my head.

'We'll get something on the way. Do you think Dave will be in the club today? It's Sunday, isn't it? I don't even know. I'm tired as well.' She talks at me. Like nothing happened last night.

'Why did that guy go mad?'

She lets go of my hand but we still walk close together. She puts her hand up and rubs the back of her head. Someone rides past on a bike.

'Thought he owned the place. Thought he paid and that meant whatever. I didn't.' She's still rubbing her head, pulling her hand through her hair.

'So you work there?'

'Course I do.' Fast, again. She speeds up so she's a

couple of steps ahead of me. I just keep walking behind her, watching her mess about with the back of her head.

In the pub my belly starts sloshing round because I can smell a bit of food. Lee's stood at the bar getting us some drinks in and getting me a sausage butty and her whatever. I'm sat in a booth in the corner but I could've sat anywhere because there's only us and a table of students and a fat guy behind the bar. Guy's got a beard. Big beard. He's smiling at Lee while she orders and I bet he's probably thinking about having a go on her. Putting his big fucking beard all over her face. I look at the lamp on the table. It's red and it's made of plastic and it's got to be one of those things that some people, like the people who come in here, think is proper fucking cool even though it looks like a toy. They've even got it screwed to the table as if it's that good someone'd nick it. Someone's wrote on the top of the table. It's sunk in a bit, scratched in with a blue Biro. *Rise up / head up / easy way no way*. Fucked if I know what it means. Bet the cunt who did it doesn't know. I hate sitting there. I can't be arsed to move. I put one of the menus over the stupid fucking writing and wait for my drink.

I don't say anything to Lee. I drink my beer and eat my scran and look around her head. I watch the guy with the beard instead. I want him to turn the music off. I want the students next to us to fuck off. Lee stops talking and eats a bit. Like a little bird. My hand's shaking a bit when I pick my pint up. When I put the glass down, it doesn't stop. It's nothing. I stare at it and it stops. I push my plate away from me to make the beard guy notice that I'm done and I want to go. Lee knows I want to go. She's got a look on her face like sad but it's not sad, more like she's got found out for something.

'Are we going or what?'

She pushes a few beans round her plate then puts her fork down and we both get up and I walk straight out but she goes to the bar to pay the bill.

At the club a black guy comes to the door eventually and doesn't say anything, just looks at us two stood there, til Lee says Dave at him and he says yes, in some weird foreign accent, then steps over to one side to let us in the door. It's dead quiet in there and it stinks like old cig smoke now. The old bird, the Chinese-looking one, is sat behind the the front desk, like someone's nailed her arse to the seat.

'Want to leave your coat?' she says. To me. Cold as shit in my T-shirt.

'You're all right.'

Lee gets in quick. 'We need to see Dave. Is he here?'

'Lee,' the old bird smiles, 'Lee.' She's nodding her head. 'He's upstairs. Don't make a mess.' She nods her head at the black guy. He's still stood by the door even though he's closed it now.

'They are cleaning.' She starts laughing at that, like some fucker's tickling her.

'They're cleaning.'

I push through the glass door into the club and Lee comes after me and I can still hear the old girl pissing her knickers til it swings shut behind us.

+

The smell of cigs gets ten times stronger through the glass, and there's sweat and booze and piss and shit and puke in it as well, and all that's hiding together under some kind of bleach and somebody's blood. A small Chinese-looking guy stops whatever he's doing behind the bar and watches us come in.

'Dave?' Lee says, and she points up at the ceiling.

'Yeah,' the guy says back, looking at me. 'Go up.'

We walk over the sticky carpet, over the sticky cracked laminate round the booth, by the stage, and start going up the stairs. Lee goes first. The guy behind the bar watches us all the way.

'What you here for again? Speak to Dave?'

I stop on the first step. Lee carries on.

'You were here the other night,' the guy says.

'Must be thinking of someone else, mate,' I say. He gets his phone out of his pocket and starts typing something, not interested in me any more. I go up the stairs. I notice that I've still got some dry blood down the front of my T-shirt. Walked into town, sat in the pub with it. No one gives a fuck. I don't know if it's mine or not.

Lee is at the top waiting for me. The lights are all on so it's pretty bright up there. It doesn't look like it did. The curtains on the stage are pulled open and there's just a few boxes behind and some stacked up chairs. There's some girl rattling bottles behind the bar and Dave is sat on one of the tables up near the front, with a black guy sat opposite him, and they're talking but the black guy doesn't look too happy. They both look over to us when we start to walk over and the black guy says something to Dave and gets up quickly so that the chair behind him goes back on two legs and nearly falls over. Then he points at Dave, right at his face and says something else. Then he storms off, past us and down the stairs. Dave is smiling the whole time. He doesn't get up for us.

'Mikey lad, and little Lee.' He's got a big grin, and he taps his hands on the table when he speaks, drumming. 'This is early. Night children you two, aren't you?' He laughs.

'We haven't got up early,' Lee says.

'No, no, course not. Up all night caning it, no doubt.' Dave gives me a little nod of the head. 'You aren't looking too great for it though, can I just drop that in?'

'Something happened, Dave. Ian's dead.' Lee's voice is shaky. 'And Alex.'

'What?' His face changes. He's stopped smiling. He stops drumming his hands. 'When? How the fuck?'

'Some guys. Broke into the club. They had a gun, Dave. They torched the place.' Lee sags down into a chair. I stay stood where I am, in between the two of them at the side of the table.

'Lynn!' Dave shouts across at the girl behind the bar. 'Fuck off for a bit, yeah?' She goes downstairs. 'And you two made it out?'

'We weren't in,' I say.

'We were in the yard. They left us,' Lee says.

'Why?' Dave says.

'Don't know. They were chasing us down. Then they

just fucked off.' Lee's got her head down. I think she might be crying again. 'It's my fault,' she says, to the table top. 'A punt got hold of me. Made out like he was going to do something to me. Michael tried to help. Stabbed him.'

'And he came back?'

'Not him. His mates? People he knows? I don't know.'

'Sounds like you stabbed the wrong fella,' Dave says to me and he sits back in his chair and he folds his arms over his belly. He looks over Lee's head, over at the stage, staring. Lee sniffs.

'7th Heaven's done then? Burnt out? You two left?'

'I reckon,' I say. The smoke was thick and black in the cold sky, when we left.

'We need somewhere, Dave. We OK here?' Lee looks up at him. Her face is wet.

Dave looks at me, then her, then back to me, then at the stage, at some point in the air. It seems like it takes him ages to say anything.

'No.'

Lee makes a noise, like she just cut herself.

'No, I don't have anywhere for you.'

I'm trying to see if he's joking, trying to look at his eyes, but he's still looking at the distance, at the pulled-back curtains. Lee keeps her head down.

'I've got nothing for you,' Dave says. 'You can't be here. You can't be anywhere near here. They know you both. They'll keep an eye out for you.'

'We're hungry, Dave.' Her voice is small but steady.

'Go, Lee.'

Lee gets up. She puts her little hands on the table, her

fingers are all spread out and white. Dave looks at her then. She turns her head up. Her hair is all hanging in her face, over her eyes but I can still see them, wide, staring him down. A tear falls off her chin onto the table. She keeps Dave locked in for a minute. Then she takes a big breath.

'Die, then,' she whispers.

She stands up straight and walks over to the stairs. She stops at the top, but she doesn't turn round. I think she's waiting for me. I go to follow her and behind me I hear Dave's chair slide across the hard floor.

'Don't come back, little Lee. Not ever.'

I get to where she is and we start down the stairs.

'I'm sorry,' Dave says, but I almost don't hear it.

26

We don't speak on the way back to the flat. Lee keeps checking her phone. I think I fall asleep for a second on the tram because I see the white room under the club and the table in the middle's got everyone's bodies stacked up on it, on top of each other. Some are burned black and some are leaking red everywhere, but I mostly just stare at Alex's battered face and her one eye that stares dead, right into me, then blinks once. I make a noise when I open my eyes and Lee looks at me, and some other people on the tram look round at me as well.

I let her go through the flat door first. Dig is in. I can hear the TV while we go upstairs, and he's shouting at something happening on his computer. I think about making a brew when we go past the kitchen door.

'Let's go quick,' Lee says.

So I don't bother. We get up to the front room and Lee sits on the edge of Dig's bed. I stand in the middle of the room.

'All right, fucksticks,' Dig says, without turning round from the screen. He's got headphones on so he speaks too loud. The TV is blasting and I turn it down.

'What do you need?' Lee says to me.

I look round the room. There's a pile of clothes on the floor behind the couch. There's a pair of trainers in the corner near the electric heater. I go to the wall and unplug my phone charger and put it in my pocket, then I go to the pile of clothes and pull out a T-shirt that hasn't got blood on and put it on, then a black hoodie on over that. I get a coat off the back of the armchair and put that on. I tap my pockets. Wallet. Keys. Phone. Lighter.

'OK,' I say. 'Laters, Dig.'

He doesn't look round.

The station is quiet. A pigeon has got in somehow and it's walking around looking for a way out but there's glass walls everywhere and it's probably confused as fuck. It stops every now and again and pecks at the floor even though I can't see anything there worth pecking at. The floor's clean. Both the pigeon's feet are fine. It gets closer to my feet. Doesn't look like a town pigeon. Lee shuffles about on the bench, and her arm brushes against me. The pigeon jumps away from us a bit, but it comes back, doing little circles but moving nearer each time. Something under the seat's got it sucked in. A bit of pasty or something. I have a look but I can't see anything down there. It circles round again and it's close enough for me to boot it one if I want. Lee stamps her foot and it flies off to the other side of the station, and it lands outside a place that sells butties for something stupid like a fiver a pop. Proper lost, the little bastard.

'Twenty minutes,' Lee says when she looks up at the big board.

'Right,' I say.

We're the only people in the carriage. Nobody's come round for tickets. Lee's got a bottle of Diet Coke on the table in front of her and she's holding it with both hands, like she doesn't want anyone taking it off her. She hasn't drank any yet. I keep seeing myself in the window, my face in the glass, coloured in by black-green bushes when they fly past.

'We're gone then.'

'Suppose,' she says.

'You know what we're doing?'

'Not really. We have to go somewhere.' She unscrews the top off the bottle and the drink fizzes up. 'There'll be others.'

'You hope.'

'Don't you?'

The train starts slowing down, and it stops in a grey station that looks the same the one we stopped in before. The platform is empty. Out the window I can see through a red metal fence into a car park, and into some old guy's car. He's sat in there on his own and his windows are steaming up. I check my phone. It's nearly twelve.

'I don't even know, Lee. I don't even know.'

The train pulls off again. I go with it. Not happy. Not sad. Not anything.

ACKNOWLEDGEMENTS

Nick Royle – Maniacs – MMU – Emma, Jen, Nathan, Rebecca, Rosa and Scott – Georgina Cullen – John Oakey.